SIMPLE DAME FAIRFAX

FAIRFAX

Anna Bransgrove

First Edition published 2015
2QT Limited (Publishing)
Settle, North Yorkshire BD24 9RH
United Kingdom
www.2qt.co.uk

Cover design Hilary Pitt
Cover images supplied by Shutterstock.com

Printed in Great Britain by
Lightning Source Limited UK

A CIP catalogue record for this book is available
from the British Library
ISBN 978-1-910077-51-1

To Mike
for your unfailing faith in the slightly deranged
gentlewoman in the parlour

Acknowledgements

My truly grateful thanks:

to Eric and Twinks for inspiring me with a love of Yorkshire and the Brontës

to Fuz for unwavering enthusiasm and encouragement and our shared love of Haworth

to Patsy for wise insights and advice, for positive reactions to the first draft of *Simple Dame Fairfax*, and especially for the scholarly Foreword which enriches this book

to Catherine Cousins, Karen Holmes and everyone at 2QT for swift, friendly and most professional guidance throughout the publishing process, and to Hilary Pitt for the cover design

and finally to Charlotte Brontë without whom my Aliz would not exist.

Contents

Foreword

By the time we meet 'simple dame Fairfax' in Charlotte Brontë's *Jane Eyre*, we are very well acquainted with Jane herself. We have shared in her Gateshead rebellion against her bullying cousin John and have felt her distress and humiliation at Mr. Brocklehurst's Lowood School. The story is Jane's autobiography, and it is through Jane's consciousness that we meet and evaluate the other actors in her tale, including Mrs. Fairfax. It is through Jane's eyes that we see 'the neatest imaginable little elderly lady, in widow's cap, black silk gown and snowy muslin apron[1]', and it is Jane who tells us that 'my heart really warmed to the worthy lady as I heard her talk' (97). Two chapters later, however, Jane has 'placed' her companion: 'Mrs. Fairfax turned out to be what she appeared, a placid-tempered, kind-natured woman, of competent education and average intelligence' (108). 'I valued what was good in Mrs. Fairfax', she tells us, 'but I believed in the existence of other and more vivid kinds of goodness, and what I believed in I wished to behold'.

Jane's frustration with her dull life at Thornfield fuels a proto-feminist outburst, recognising that 'millions are condemned to a stiller doom than mine, and millions are in silent revolt against their lot'. Women, she insists, 'suffer from too rigid a restraint, too absolute a stagnation, precisely as men would suffer' (109). It is only when Mr. Rochester arrives that

---

1 Charlotte Brontë, *Jane Eyre* [1847]. Oxford World's Classics, 2008, p. 95. Further references will be to this edition.

she glimpses through him something of the 'vivid … goodness' she has craved: 'I had a strange delight', she tells us, 'in receiving the new ideas he offered, in imagining the new pictures he portrayed, and following him in thought through the new regions he disclosed' (146). Mrs. Fairfax becomes irrelevant as Rochester 'was becoming to me my whole world' (274). Rochester, equally engrossed with Jane, takes 'simple dame Fairfax' for granted (249), while Jane 'impatiently' rejects her warning that 'gentlemen in his station are not accustomed to marry their governesses' (265).

Jane Eyre is sometimes called a 'romance' or a 'gothic tale', but it captures our attention mainly through its realism. Its picturing of external detail – the window-seat at Gateshead, the gooseberry pie she helps to make at Moor House – creates a believable physical environment, while its sharp evocation of anger or grief works to convey psychological truth. Yet Henry James points out that all such realist pictures involve a sleight of hand. Realism creates the illusion that the places, people and events represented in a novel – what George Eliot called 'this particular web' – is continuous with 'that tempting range of relevancies called the universe'[2]. Thornfield Hall lies near the village of Hay; further off is the larger town of Millcote, and by implication the rest of England lies beyond. Adèle's mother, Cèline, is represented in a single incident, yet we assume that the life of Paris, with its theatres and boulevards, lies around her. The first Mrs. Rochester's early life occupies a few brief pages, yet they suggest not only its different climate and social milieu, but also an unbroken chain of relations linking that Caribbean island with Thornfield Hall.

These 'suggestions', 'implications' and 'assumptions' about relations with the larger world are an essential part of the novelist's art. As James puts it, 'really, universally, relations stop nowhere, and the exquisite problem of the artist is eternally but to draw, by a geometry of his own, the circle within which

---

2 George Eliot, *Middlemarch* (1871), Ch. XV.

they shall happily *appear* to do so'.[3] The illusion depends on the characters at the centre of the circle being more vivid and detailed than those who are further away, who can be sketched or merely 'suggested'. The 'circle' of *Jane Eyre* has Jane herself as its centre, but if we shift that focal point to another character within her story, another circle can be drawn, overlapping but not identical with hers, deriving its vividness from 'an alternative centre of self, whence the lights and shadows must always fall with a certain difference'.[4]

Anna Bransgrove's novella draws this different circle, taking as its centre 'simple dame Fairfax', the woman who appears in *Jane Eyre* as part of the realist furniture but who proves, in this new story, to have her own web of connections with the world, and her own 'lights and shadows'. Like *Jane Eyre*, Bransgrove's story has a realist framework. Mrs. Fairfax is the housekeeper at Thornfield Hall, and her story is shaped by the house which is both her home and her occupation. Each chapter is named after a room in the house, or a place nearby, and, as in *Jane Eyre*, its detail persuades us of the reality of the housekeeper's life, as she makes the blackcurrant cordial or stitches the drawing-room cushions. This Mrs. Fairfax, however, is no cipher. She has given names – Alice Elizabeth – and she has an inner life.

Her story unfolds in the interval after Jane's escape from Thornfield, when both Jane and Rochester are absent from the house, leaving Alice in possession of the rooms and the memories they evoke. Her life in this suspended moment is emblematic of her life in general, since she has 'always found myself in the middle, caught between extremes, a still, placid fulcrum, or so I may appear, to the powerful heavy forces on each side of me'. Though the tone of her narration is quiet, understated, we gradually learn of forces, heavy enough, which have acted on her own life and compelled her into 'stagnation'. In accepting her place at Thornfield as a refuge

3 Henry James, *The Art of the Novel*. New York and London: Scribner's Sons, 1934, p. 5.
4 *Middlemarch*, Ch. XXI.

9

from past betrayals, she has accepted that 'stiller doom' which Jane deplores. As the details of her past emerge we see that Bransgrove is teasing new stories, new relations, from what we know of Jane's world, both augmenting and inventing so that what overlaps with Charlotte Brontë's novel gives that story new depth, and what appears in the unknown arc of this new circle is meshed with what we know already, exploiting the link with *Jane Eyre* to maintain the realist illusion that 'this particular web' is infinitely linked to a larger whole.[5]

As Alice goes about her daily life, performing the domestic functions for which she is paid, her mind is free to revisit scenes from the past – griefs which are unsuspected by readers of *Jane Eyre* but which explain her presence at Thornfield, where she and Rochester are bound by mutual secrets. As she works, the present scene repeatedly recedes to allow other pictures and voices to inhabit her mind, and this continual fading from present to past is more than a narrative device to tell her life story. Alice's recollections soon become 'visitations', an involuntary absorption in the past which threatens her self-possession. As Rochester returns from his fruitless search for Jane, Alice is shocked to find that his new obsession overrides his old kindness and that she is to be betrayed once more. In an accelerating narrative, past and present rush together. Her memories become 'poisoned', the burden of her secrets more than she can bear, her role as a 'still, placid fulcrum' no longer tenable. The last pages surprise us with her 'silent revolt'.

Dr Patsy Stoneman
Emeritus Reader in English, University of Hull
Vice President of the Brontë Society
February 2015

---

5 *Middlemarch*, Ch. XIV.

1

DOORWAY

So, she has run away after all, the governess. I am not surprised. When the truth came out I knew how it would be and she acted true to form. Correct, self-righteous to the end.

Even before I met her I knew the person she was. As soon as I read my name on her first letter, written in that neat, faultless hand, the edges of the paper turned in evenly, just so, I understood what she was. There was no surprise when we met. Small, plain, Quakerish. But with a sharp light in those short-sighted eyes.

He has just called out. Leah is to bring brandy to the library (which was, for some months, the governess's schoolroom). I watch from my parlour doorway as she leaves him to his glass and decanter and makes her way back to the kitchen. I hear him turn the key in the lock and I hesitate, waiting, without purpose. Perhaps he will call for me, summon me to sit awhile with him, though he has no reason to do so and he will not care for my inconsequential chatter. But I would be content to keep him company, quietly busy with my needlework by the fireside. I understand rejection. Maybe I could turn his mind from his loss – but no! That is not possible. I am growing foolish as I age even to entertain such a notion.

None the less I find myself close beside the library door, my hand raised to knock, with the forgotten childhood name, Teddy, almost escaping from my dry lips.

How can this be? Is it that in the storm and fury of yesterday's shameful exposure I saw only empty disappointment in his eyes? Saw again an eight-years' child, his rejection stark and naked, when his elder brother disregarded him, sent him packing with a curt, 'Run along home, you baby!'

…And turned to me…

The clink of a glass breaks my memory. I hear the leathery thwack as the dog shakes himself, the click of his claws on the wooden floor, and the flop of his weight as he re-settles on the mat in front of the hearth.

'Lie still, Pilot!' The harsh voice chokes on a stifled sob.

I turn away and scurry up the wide hallway. I do not like to be so close to this raw grief and am suddenly ashamed of myself, skulking in doorways, listening at keyholes.

2

STILL ROOM

I could not rest last night and spent the leaden hours muddled and trapped midway between my own old sadness and our present turmoil. There is a tight band of pain around my tired head but I am busy in the still room, making cordial from the currants which have quickly ripened in this hot summer sunshine. Leah picked half a bushel before breakfast this morning and brought them to me. Since I first came here I have always made the currant cordial. I will continue to do so. Why should anything change – even after the revelations of two days ago?

As I stand at the scrubbed white deal table, the currants glowing in the basket on my left, the sugar block stark to my right, and I in the middle with the scales and weights ranged ready, I pause. It seems to me that I have always found myself in the middle, caught between extremes, a still, placid fulcrum, or so I may appear, to the powerful heavy forces on each side of me. Even my name, the name Rowland gave me when I was little more than a child, the name by which I know myself, is a cipher indicating my situation.

…'Alice Elizabeth,' he says slowly, savouring its flavour. 'What a mouthful! Too much for such a small, dainty little body as you have grown to be.' He smiles as he speaks, his eyes creasing at the corners. I let my gaze fall as he confronts me, watching his full lips as he speaks again.

"'Aliz", that's who you are.' He pauses. His words are a caress.

'My Aliz.' And there I am, re-christened by the unchristian man, caught between the beginning and the end of the alphabet, midway between all words…

I weigh out the fruit, calculate the proportion of sugar, dig my hands deep into the berries until the juices burst and my fingers are stained with crimson streaks. I take the soft white muslin, drape the earthenware bowl, place it on the cool stone shelf and leave it there for its allotted time.

Washing my hands, watching the colour seep into the water, I recognise that at my housewifely task I am no housewife; nor am I cook or servant; neither have I ever been guest in this great house.

My place has always been indeterminate, midway between kept and keeper.

3

DRAWING ROOM

He has stamped out of the house, half drunk, angry, close to tears, calling John to saddle Mesrour. I believe he did not even see me as he flung on his cloak and I handed him his whip which had fallen on the floor.

'Make haste, John,' he bellowed, adding to himself in a rapid, reiterated kind of chant that heard no reply, 'How long has she been gone? How long since she left me? How long?'

It is two days now since they were closeted for hours together. Two days since I sat in my parlour patiently, listening, waiting, hearing nothing but the voice in my head saying (as I knew *she* would) that she was too fine, too independent, too essentially pure to be a kept woman. Too proud to submit to his patronage, too stubborn to lean on his protection.

Silly girl! What value have such notions when passions burn? None at all. I know. I remember...

> ...Clouds in a blue sky and an oak tree above me. Green moss beneath. And his breath, his lips, his hands. Rowland!...

Yesterday, in those long, waiting hours, Rowland's brother must have asked her to stay, begged, pleaded. She should have lain down beside him, for him, then and there. Never to leave.

> ...As I did for Rowland, with the oak-leaf curtain above me.
> I would have stayed, cleaved to him. Always.
> But he did not beg me to stay...

I watched him as he made his way to the stable block, his stride unsteady, his voice ringing out across the yard.

'She shall not leave me like this. I'll fetch her back. God damn me if I don't!'

I do not like to see him raging thus. There is no dignity in the man. He is degraded by his grief. And it is she who has done this to him.

And so, I turn and go back inside the Hall, about my duties as if nothing untoward has happened. As if no governess had ever come here to disrupt our even lives. Granted, it has never been easy here, but we have sustained a kind of order and conformity (in spite of the unspoken things) which has pleased me over the years.

No one can ever say that I have neglected the Hall or failed to keep the reception rooms spic and span, even when I had no reason to expect Mr. Edward's return. In silent spring times and weary winters I have arranged the cleaning and refurbishment, whenever they have been required. No – *before* they have been required, I should say. I pride myself on keeping a step ahead of mould or moth hole, tarnish or filmy swathe of dust.

Silence echoes throughout the house today but there is no reason for me to shirk my duties. Why should I? I have never scanted my guardianship.

Some of the purple cushions are starting to fade a little, I notice, here in the drawing room, and the deep velvet curtains over the archway that leads to the dining room do not hang quite evenly. A hook has come adrift, I suspect.

Will he open his house again, I wonder. Host another house party, as he did last summer? I think not. Now that the secret is out, it cannot be. We shall be shunned by our neighbours, excluded from our acquaintanceship, the scandal infecting us as if we had caught a pestilence which all fear. I dare say there will be no more house parties.

I remember how I helped her to ensconce herself in this alcove, before the ladies left the dining table, when we were summoned to attend. The talk among the servants had taken a new turn; Miss Ingram was to be their next mistress, it was commonly agreed. John and Leah laughed at me when I said I thought otherwise, though they had tittle-tattled all through the spring time, calling their master moon-struck and bewitched, Leah and Betsey repeatedly wondering what he could see in the governess's pigmy stature, her straight, mouse-brown hair and her knowing look.

But I had been the first to see it as it was, on the very first occasion when she was summoned to this room. I recollect, she followed after me in her austere black gown, as if she clung to my shadow. She had not thought to wear her single piece of jewellery (that modest pearl brooch, a mere trinket) until I prompted her. Wasn't she aware of the respect due to her master?

I saw him fix his eyes on the child and the dog, deliberately keeping his gaze from her, it seemed to me. It irked me somewhat that she looked so perfectly assured, but then she always did. I never saw her out of countenance, not even on Tuesday last, either when they returned from the church, or up aloft, afterwards. I have to give her that. Her composure was always commendable. As was mine, of course.

That evening, sitting with his injured ankle resting on a cushioned stool, he questioned her, ordered her to play for him. She did not lie when she said she played 'a little'. I have an ear for music and it must be said that she was merely competent. I sat apart with my knitting, tea having been dispensed, and I heard that the notes were accurate, well practised. There was, however, something mechanical in their execution. How stiffly she sat at the forte piano, her fingers moving skilfully enough, the tempo strictly measured. But there was no passion in her performance. He soon stopped her in mid phrase, and the interrupted notes hung in the air as she bent to offer him her portfolio at his request.

Perhaps there was passion in the paintings. I know not. They did not appeal to me. Gloomy of hue, and each with something macabre or melancholy in their subject matter. Two minutes would have been sufficient time for me to appraise them. He, however, took longer. And he questioned her at length about them, too. There was an intensity in him, as he sat there, very different from his habitual brooding. Since the night he returned here after his father's death, I had never seen his morbid gloominess leave him. Not until he clapped eyes on the governess, that is.

I spoke up for her that evening, as I recall, saying she taught the young French girl well, and was companionable to me. And scant thanks I got for my commendation – from him or from her.

And their conversation! Well I never! Men in green and moonlit revels! I could not make head nor tale of much of it, though I guessed soon enough at the meaning of their unspoken words. It was the governess herself who prompted me. No sooner had we been dismissed than she began her inquisition into his 'strange nature'. What was his history? What painful thoughts filled his mind and aroused his moods? Oh! she was eager, indeed, in her questioning. And as to the family troubles that I hinted at? She was not to be fobbed off with generalities. I had to think fast to speak the truth and hide the truth and satisfy her interrogation at one and the same time.

In my answers I recollect that I had to glance at Rowland's part in it all. I believe I said he and his father had been not quite just to Mr. Edward. That he had been placed in an uncongenial situation and a breach had occurred. That would do, I thought. She would have to accept that he found the Hall gloomy. It was all that I was prepared to say. I believe she recognized my evasions but I would say no more. In my heart I knew she would do well to meddle no further.

And in my heart I knew that I was powerless to hinder that from happening.

4

THE LEADS

More than two weeks have passed and he has not returned; nor am I to expect him unless he is fortunate in his search. A letter from him, which I received this morning, lists instructions which I am to carry out with all haste.

> *'Instruct Mamzelle to pack her bags and prepare for her return to France at the end of next week. I require her services no more. Should my return be prolonged until after her departure I request you to pay her £15 at the curtailment of her employment.*
>
> *Adele Varens is to commence attending Miss Lebberston's School in Stokesley as a permanent boarding pupil this day week.*
>
> *Kindly supervise all arrangements for her packing and departure.'*

So, I have had occasion to visit the boxroom on the second floor this morning, to find suitable trunks and boxes for the little French girl's requirements. Poor child! She has been sadly distressed by recent events, and though she may not understand all that has occurred, I feel sure that her *bonne* will have relished gossiping to her about it. I have grown fond of Adele in recent months, and find her demeanour and manner much improved.

Decidedly different from the flighty little doll who was fledged upon us, almost eighteen months ago, speaking only to Sophie in her gibberish tongue. Doubtless, removal from the dissipations of Paris and transplantation to this quiet corner of Yorkshire proved doubly beneficial but, I must admit, much of her improvement may be attributed to the influence of her governess. Who, it must also be said, never even bade the child farewell.

Once the trunk and band box were selected, I climbed the ladder beyond the narrow attic staircase, raised the trapdoor and, with no little difficulty, pulled myself through the square aperture into the daylight and up here onto the leads once again.

I brought *her* here, I recall, when her first morning's work was over and Sophie had taken the prattling French girl for her walk. A tour of the reception rooms and first-floor chambers, followed by a walk in the grounds, would have sufficed as her introduction to the Hall. What was it that made me conduct her to the third storey, with its antiquated furnishings and shadowy doorways? I knew its dangers, just as I knew many of its secrets. What prompted me to lead her here I cannot say, but perhaps I sensed a danger even then, and some perversity within me could not resist drawing her towards it.

I remember the thrill that ran through my blood as I took her past that particular secluded doorway. Even then, eleven months ago as near as I can estimate, it was no easy thing for me to climb the stepladder at the end of the gloomy corridor, unbolt the trapdoor on its massy hinges, to haul myself out onto the roof. Yet I did just that, as I have done again, now.

Everywhere this morning there is a damp grey mist beneath flat grey clouds. Last time, the sun was shining, surprisingly hot on that autumn day. I watched her as she trod across the leads, her neat little foot padding over the very place where the other was concealed. I watched her lean forward between the dark stone crenellations, as I am leaning now, and look first down and then out, and across the grounds and fields to the hills beyond.

Then I stood by the trapdoor, watching, as she turned her eyes to follow the flight of a rook, its cawing voice jeering through the morning air. What was she thinking? A smug little smile lit her pale face for a moment as she looked back at an unremarkable grey-haired woman, fluttering her handkerchief before her face after her exertions.

She went ahead of me, down the ladder and the garret staircase and along the narrow passageway. I had some trouble with the bolts of the trapdoor, I recall, which delayed me. When I caught up with her she was standing motionless, her head on one side, listening intently to – for – something. She had heard laughter, she said, and was intrigued. I called for Grace and reprimanded her for levity, reminding her to remember her directions. She nodded in her usual, taciturn way and re-entered her place of work. I forestalled further questions from the young Miss. She had been avid in her interrogations about a ghost and hauntings on our tour of the third storey and I thought it best to deflect her thoughts. Luckily, like all born governesses, she could not resist an opportunity to talk of her pupil's progress under her direction, even on that first morning, and so the moment passed and life resumed its normal course, with luncheon laid out ready for us in my parlour.

5

PARLOUR

In spite of having much to do in preparation for Adele's removal, I have found time to search out sufficient matching damask to replace the drawing room cushions. There was a bolt of material in the linen press on the first floor landing. I remember wrapping it up in paper and saving it – what – eight years ago, for a time when it should be required. And so, this afternoon, before I work again on the cushion covers, I sit in my parlour stitching, turning down the hems of the girl's dresses, letting out seams, and lengthening the sleeves with deeper cuffs. She has grown considerably over the summer.

Anyone catching sight of me would see me habitually employed, a respectable elderly lady about her normal business. As always I am wryly amused by that notion, but I am bound to admit that there is a comfort in the conformity of my life. Respectability has its rewards.

I settle my concentration onto the mundane practicalities of my needlework. It gratifies me that my stitching is as neat as ever, but my fingers ache and are clumsy as I work. I am unaccountably weary. I break off from my tedious task and walk slowly through to the drawing room where the archway curtain hangs straight again. John fetched the stepladder as I asked and Leah has climbed up and replaced the hook. Methodically I remove the faded covers from the cushions ready for the new ones to be slipped on when they are finished.

Is there anything else to be done? Is that a threadbare patch on the Turkey carpet – there, four-square in front of the marble hearth? I stoop to see more clearly. Yes, a tell-tale flattening of texture, a hint of fading in the fabric; it is a little worn. There is a fine Aubusson rug in the library, behind the desk. That would suffice. I will tell John to lift it tomorrow and place it in front of the fire, here, to guard against further deterioration.

As I turn to leave the room I catch sight of a grey-haired dame in the looking glass over the mantelpiece. She has an anxious, thoughtful expression and for a split second I wonder who she is, before I see myself and am astonished that I am grown so old. I sigh. I scold myself for my fond stupidity and return to my duties.

6

HAY LANE

Tired, dispirited, I can sit no longer and as evening falls I leave the house to pace for a while, through the laurel walk, past the splintered horse chestnut and on into the orchard.

An unseasonal low mist hangs about the tree trunks and it seems to me that three figures are approaching from the distance, indistinguishable, though I know full well who they are.

...They are closer now, and I hear laughter. The central figure, the girl, eleven, twelve years old at most, smiles up at the tall young man who strides in the summer sunlight beside her. She lifts her brown skirts a little and runs a few quick steps to stay beside him. Then she turns, holding out her hand for the child, stocky, treading firmly on his sturdy legs, but fractious as the older ones outstrip him 'Teddy!' she calls softly to him, encouraging. 'Come, hold my hand.'

He stamps his boots and paces faster. 'Don't want *your* hand,' he insists. 'Roly, Roly, wait for me. Wait. I'm coming.'

And with defiance he runs past the girl, almost reaches his brother who, seeing him out of the corner of his eye, merely lengthens his stride and leaves the boy, aggrieved, angry, impotent on the pathway behind him.

'Run along home, you baby,' he taunts, and looks straight at the girl. 'Leave him,' he says, and then, tempting her, 'Come with me.' And he is off, running between the bent apple trees, stopping, waiting until she has almost reached him, when he laughs and takes off again.

Breathless, she pursues him once more and this time he pretends to stumble, lets her catch up with him, and as she kneels beside him he takes her hand and says, suddenly quiet and intimate, as if bestowing a gift, 'Look here, here, Alice Elizabeth,' and points to a gnarled tree trunk festooned with grey, feathery lichen above which one, two, three dozy wasps hover and glide before they wriggle their way into a crack in the wood. 'A wasp's nest,' he says. 'There will be thousands of wasps in there. Countless wasps. Are you frightened?'

She shakes her head, unable to speak the lie.

'Watch!' he orders.

And slowly he rises to his feet, lifts his leather-booted foot, raises his knee, high, pauses and stamps down, down, as the girl turns and flees, scampers across the uneven grass, the sound of his laughter ringing across the orchard...

This evening the grass is strewn with ungathered apples. I stoop to pick one up, am about to raise it to my lips when I feel a spongy mush beneath my fingertips, see a blackened circle enclosing a tiny hole from which – a stifled cry slips from my lips as I drop the rotting fruit – an earwig pokes its sharp bronzed head and wiry forelegs. Shuddering, I cross to the orchard gate, admonishing myself for being repelled by a simple insect going about its business of prolonging its existence. What was I thinking of to be so foolish as to pick up rotting windfall fruit? I should have known better.

Latching the gate behind me, I step down the bank and walk along the path until I reach the stile at the edge of Hay Lane. The dog roses are all faded now and the white convolvulus petals are tarnished in dusk's dampness. Dried grass heads wave frail, shorn spikes, their thin stems brittle. A few scattered leaves splinter under my feet as I walk. There is suddenly a chill of autumn on the air. All too soon, the early frosts will bite again, startling us with their brief intensity, reminding us of winter's grasp.

It was hard winter when they met.

Strange, disturbing for me, that it should have been here, near the stile in Hay Lane, that he chanced upon her. I lean for a moment against the stile now. I am weary and the familiar ache in the bones of my neck sends sparks of pain upwards into my skull. Looking about me at the shadowy lane my thoughts follow a track of their own – and I remember…

> …waiting here on an August evening, eager at first, alert for footstep or hoof beat, turning my head at every sound, then anxious, imagining accidents or disasters, later fretful, aggrieved. Finally despondent, knowing with a chill, hollow lunge of despair that I had been duped, disregarded, cast away. Knowing that Rowland was not going to come to me… Knowing also that I had especial need of him…

The mist is rising, seeping up the valley, the Hall almost invisible in a veil of vapour. On its filmy strands the past floats before my eyes, which I realise are heavy with unshed tears. But I will not cry. I will not. I have no cause. Or no more cause than has been mine for so many long years. The imagined promises, the hopes and the hard realities hurt me sorely enough all those years ago. I should have cried my full ere now.

7

CHURCH

Ignoring the whispers of the congregation who, for all I know are still re-living the startling events which took place here, what is it? more than a month ago, I am in my usual pew at St Saviour's church. When I was a child my place was in the fifth row from the front on the left-hand side, my family's place. Somewhere near the middle of the church, of course, where a respectable farmer's family should rightfully be. Not at the front in the carved oak pews with their embroidered hassocks on the carpeted floor; nor yet at the back, in the pine benches where the rough kneelers, rickety on the flagstones, creak, as the labourers and servants bow their heads and mumble their responses.

The smell is the same as it always is: beeswax, candle grease, dust, mouse droppings, damp. Nothing here has changed though so many significant things have happened within these grey stone walls over the centuries: the destruction of images, fervent avowals, funerals, marriages.

And sometimes, even in my own flicker of a lifetime, travesties of those.

My present place is, as it has been for the last fifteen years, next to the aisle, on the right-hand side, in the third of the rows ascribed to the Rochester family. But between the time of my childhood and before I came to live at Thornfield, I had another place, which was rightfully mine. I played my allotted part there. I wrapped my secret up beneath my neatly attired body, under its sprigged or ribbonned or furred bonnet (as befitted each season) and took to reading my bible as a vicar's wife should. Yes, Sunday became the lodestone of my week.

How apposite. Yet no one knew or guessed or even paused to consider why I attended the services so dutifully – no, more than that – so fervently. There was, you see, always a possibility of that special blessing – a glance of acknowledgement or a word of recognition from Rowland, if he were not travelling elsewhere or about his business, wasting or expanding his fortune in London or some other great commercial city.

And when he was from home, which he was most frequently, I would focus my eyes not on Lionel's bland, weak face as he led the prayers or spoke his sermon but on the old man in the first Rochester pew. I would search for a glimpse of likeness in the father of the son. Then my spirit filled with a hungry longing while my respectable ordinary body knelt and rose, sang hymns and intoned responses, as was customary.

And that longing has always smouldered inside me. It has been with me, part of me, for too long. Even at the moment of my delight, as my love sparked into life when he first looked at me, I knew that he drew me to him as surely as a candle's flame draws a moth. And, trapped between pain and pleasure, danger and delight, I had no power to draw back into the safety of the shadows.

8

THE RECTORY

Since I was a young woman it has always been my practice to keep myself well away from tittle-tattle and gossip and I have certainly not changed my habits in recent months. However, I could not escape from having a full account of the governess's interrupted wedding from Rev. Wood's housekeeper when I called at the rectory this afternoon to enquire about the whereabouts of a reliable chimney sweep. Since old Thaddeus Mills suffered his seizure last May he has been unable to resume work, his left side being weakened and useless much as I remember my poor father's was. The Thornfield chimneys are sorely in need of sweeping before winter sets in and Mrs. Chepstow recommends Jack Dyer from Gunnerdale village, a few miles west of Hay. I have sent word to him, trusting that he will be eager for work at so great a mansion as Thornfield Hall.

Mrs. Chepstow invited me to prolong my visit and take tea with her, which I was well disposed to do. I like to return to the Rectory from time to time and it always pleases me, as I sit in the kitchen with the housekeeper, to remember that I was mistress of that solid, spacious house for nigh on ten years.

Naturally I never allude to my former position and indeed,

our conversation this afternoon was of far more recent events. Mrs. Chepstow had all the details from Rev. Wood himself, and relished re-telling the tale. In spite of myself I could not resist picturing the occasion as she recounted it. I could well imagine the vicar's expression when the ceremony was stopped so suddenly by the London lawyer. Stephen Wood has inherited his father's pale green eyes and has an habitually startled expression, always putting me in mind of a young leveret surprised by a lurcher. I imagine that the reverend's appearance at the moment when the service was so abruptly stopped might have been a cause for merriment had not the events themselves been so serious.

And Mr. Rochester himself! How he looked! Mrs. Chepstow told me that Rev. Wood confided in her that he was reminded of a painting of the damned being thrust down into the pit of the Inferno, which he had seen as a child when visiting some Gothic minster in the wild marshes of Suffolkshire. The frowning, tortured visage of one particular lost soul had terrified his dreams as a child and lived with him all his adult life; indeed, had so impressed him that it had had no little influence in guiding him to devote his life to the service of the Almighty as a man of the cloth. And this ghastly stare had plagued him with renewed force when he witnessed Edward Rochester's agony as he confronted his accusers and made his confession in our little parish church last August.

Mrs. Chepstow's chair creaked under her heavy frame as she leant forward and fanned herself with her apron, her round cheeks flushed and her breathing shallow and irregular as she recounted her tale. But while I nodded and sipped my tea and prompted her with questions to continue, my mind slid away from the governess's interrupted nuptials, to events of nigh on a quarter of a century ago, at the same altar rails in the same Norman church, to another parody of a marriage. For a moment I smothered the thought while the housekeeper chattered on, echoing Mr. Mason's avowal of the lawyer's claims, declaring that Rev. Wood had feared that Mr. Rochester would strike out and fell both lawyer and brother-in-law when the accusation was first made.

But no matter how I schooled myself while her words bubbled on, I found it impossible to clear from my mind images of that other day, that other ceremony, no less unorthodox in the intention of the man who stood as bridegroom, no more binding in its consummation, than the governess's fractured wedding service.

> ...he stands, boldly, holding out his hand, the breadth of his body blotting out the slanting light which filters through the green stained glass like sunlight through leaves. Holding out his hand ... he beckons ... draws the girl-woman close ... there ... before the very altar table. He is laughing, his eyes glassy with sparks of merriment. In spite of herself she feels the smile softening her lips...

Mrs. Chepstow is looking at me with a fixed and reflective gaze. Perhaps I have smiled at an inappropriate moment in her narrative. I arrange my features, look attentive. She appears to be waiting for me to speak. Perhaps she attributes my silence, my air of abstraction, to my deafness, which I own, has become more severe of late though the voices inside my head are louder, clearer than ever. She clears her throat and asks me what I think of it all and, with a determined effort, I ask of the governess, how she looked; was she faint? And the housekeeper is off again, praising the disappointed bride's composure, exclaiming as to her pallor, approving her silence as she stared upwards at the man she would marry.

> ...The girl looks up at the broad-shouldered man.
> 'For sport, Aliz,' he says aloud, his warm, deep laughter ringing down the chancel. 'I dare you, Aliz. If you love me as you say you do, you will

34

not falter. Come.' And he takes from his pocket a plaited chain of daisies, their petals tipped with a blush of pink, which they had picked from the sward beneath the oak tree, and he slips it on her finger and twists it round and round. 'There, now. I declare you wife to me,' he says, laughter breaking the rhythm of the words. She whispers, asking is there anything she should say or do, but he stops her words. 'Say nothing. Not a thing at all. All is said – and done – already!'

The rushing words are dancing round her, the questions like flames, the doubts smoking in the air. But he takes her in his arms and kisses her, bruising her lips with his ardour and she falls against him helpless there, arch and stone around them spinning away, till there is nothing in the world but their desire.

'Done already – and will be done again,' he breathes, and even at that moment as he stretches her out on the worn carpet before the font, she closes her ears so that she will not hear the mocking triumph in his voice…

When I rose to leave, Mrs. Chepstow pressed on me a flask of her camomile cordial. I was looking tired and worn she said, and no doubt the shocking events have proved distressing for us all at Thornfield Hall. The cordial would help me sleep, she added. And was it true that Mr. Rochester was still scouring Yorkshire in search of Miss Eyre? After all this time? And what of the locked-up wife in the attic? His wife of fifteen years? How much had she heard and understood of the proceedings and what was to become of her?

At this stream of questions I took my cue from her concern for my well-being and hastened to bring the conversation to an end, saying I knew nothing to suggest that there would be any change in the arrangements for the care of Mrs. Rochester and pleading weariness and the need to return to my own fireside before dusk fell. No, I could not say anything with certainty about Mr. Rochester's intentions. Perhaps he would return to the Continent, I ventured, and, thanking the housekeeper for the restorative cordial, I made my farewells and took the path across the park land.

Nearing the Hall I saw through the gloaming the slight figure of the little French girl at the library window. I raised my hand in greeting but she made no response, merely continuing her gaze as the sky darkened and shadows lengthened along the avenue.

9

PARLOUR

Perhaps Mrs. Chepstow's cordial does indeed possess soporific powers, for I slept more soundly last night and woke refreshed for the first time since the turmoil of the wedding-day revelations.

How quiet the house is as I eat my solitary lunch. John brought the coach to the door early this morning and Sophie and the girl left before eight o'clock struck. They spend tonight at Northallerton and journey to Stokesley tomorrow. After which the French woman will make her way to the south coast, thence by packet to the Continent and her native town.

It surprises me that I miss Adele's company, I who so often looked askance at her flightiness and had frequent cause to reprimand her for boisterousness or levity, behaviour which now appears to me as mere juvenile high spirits. Her last days here, however, were quiet enough in all conscience. If she were not actually weeping, her tears were never far away and it touched my heart as I walked home yesterday to see her leaning against the window frame, scanning the driveway and beyond, hoping for a sight of her governess or her guardian's return.

Before she took her leave this morning, I spoke kindly to the child and would have caressed her but she shrugged away from my arms, and requested only that I should write and inform her *immediatement* when there was news of 'little Miss Aiyre'.

The governess's influence works strongly upon the girl, I can see. And I was not to be considered as a substitute.

Leah has brought me the *Northern Record* and an advertisement on the front page catches my eye. I can hardly believe what I see and put on my spectacles to assure myself that I have not misread the words. No, it is as I thought, as I feared. He has broadcast his shame by an inquiry, a public appeal for information.

Any person having knowledge of the whereabouts of Miss Jane Eyre on or since Wednesday 30th July is requested immediately to inform E.F.R. c/o The George and Dragon, Helmerby, North Riding of Yorkshire, a sum of 5gs being payable to any person or persons whose information elicits the discovery of the lady's present whereabouts.

I find my cheeks are flushed with embarrassment. What a hold she has over our proud master that he can demean himself so far as to publish his search for her so blatantly. I acknowledge that I am irritated, annoyed by her actions, but the strength of the anger I feel amazes me. I am caught up by the thought that during the time that has passed since her disappearance I have come not merely to criticize or question my master's actions but, because of the pain her desertion has inflicted on her lover, to feel a fierce and growing anger towards Miss Eyre. Is it possible that I *hate* the governess?

But it was not always so. I liked her well enough at first, was prepared to befriend her, might even, in those days before Mr. Rochester's return last winter, have come to think of her as something akin to a daughter. It was she, not me, who raised a barrier, not visible but strong as any drystone wall, a boundary over which I should not step.

I caught her looking at me once, in the early days, whilst I was placidly occupied with making jellies and I remember being surprised to detect – of all emotions – *pity*, in her regard. I had thought to treat her kindly, to put this virtually penniless woman at her ease, to stand in place of friends and family whom she declared were estranged from her. And yet it seemed she found my presence tedious and irksome, believed herself my superior in some unaccountable way. Even when I spoke of Mr. Rochester, who interested her beyond the commonplace, there was something in the way she bent her head as she listened and smiled knowingly to herself, which made me think that in my answers I had fallen short of some expectation which she had and which I did not understand.

But she never knew or guessed. Once she had met Mr. Edward she had no more interest in me. It never crossed her mind that I had to guard my tongue when I spoke of him and his history. Knowing nothing of my secrets, she could not imagine that I knew Rowland's brother more truly and closely than anyone at Thornfield Hall. Clever little miss that she was, she had not the wit to recognise my evasions, to appreciate the finesse in my frankness. It would have astonished her had she understood the part I played, or discovered that for all the protestations and avowals of eternal love he had made to her, it was I, simple dame Fairfax, who knew his secret: a secret which he did not have the courage to share with her.

10

PARLOUR

Days, weeks have passed and there is still no word from the master and no expectation of his return, though there is nothing unusual in that; it has often been characteristic of him to arrive at Thornfield unannounced. I wonder where his search has driven him and whether he has news of the governess's whereabouts, or whether the trail is cold.

What can she have done with herself? Where can she have gone, I wonder. She has no relatives in this country, that I know, and I believe has no friends from the orphanage she attended to whom she could turn. And indeed, what respectable person would take her in, her name and reputation compromised as they have been.

But how will she support herself? She has no references, and took only scant possessions in her hand valise. She cannot have had much money with her. It will be expedient for her to find some position as soon as possible. Perhaps she will write requesting me to vouch for her in a new position as governess again, or as companion, or – I laugh as I imagine it, the sound jumping through the silence of my parlour like a door banging on a March morning – as a housekeeper!

I find myself laughing again, gurgling, giggling at the thought of her time being spent in counting jars of preserves and hiring domestic help, not in conversation with her employer about painting or music or Men in Green! I press my fingers over my mouth to stifle my laughter and steady myself with the thought that, wherever she finds a position, she will have to attend Sunday service with the other employees and take her rightful place and keep her eyes down and behave with rectitude. I would like to see how well she can act that part. Will she match up to my performances? I think she might. And, who knows, a bespectacled and pale-complexioned curate might fancy himself in love with her and, if he hears nothing of her dubious recent history, might propose marriage.

Strange to imagine that, guarding her secret, she could one day live in some village rectory and kneel in her allotted church pew, as I did.

And that she will no more take her place as Mistress of Thornfield Hall than I have ever done.

11

DRAWING ROOM

It seems to have taken me an unconscionable time but today, at last, I have finished my needlework and have replaced the damask cushion covers. As I look out of the drawing-room window I see John gathering up wood from the fractured horse-chestnut tree. He is dragging the bigger branches towards the barn where he will chop them and stack them, leaving them to dry for at least a full year. Two years is better, he always says, and he is right. The winter fires burn best and the hearth is no trouble for Leah to clean when seasoned wood is used. But oak is best of all.

How strange the old tree looks, its massy trunk split by Midsummer Eve's lightning, its branches stark, grotesque, in their white splintered form.

Midsummer Eve. She thought me shocked when I watched them run through the storm together into the house. Saw them embrace and cling, caress and kiss as though they would drink down each other's very essence. She broke away from him before she caught my eye, a reproving hand raised to fend him off as if he were some presumptuous churl. Silly creature, even at that beating moment she contemplated rectitude and niceties of conventionality. In that second's glance she smiled, looked knowing, teasing, more than happy – triumphant!

No doubt she thought me disapproving of her. The truth was somewhat different. Surprising me with its intensity, what I felt most of all was a burning heat, a glowing longing for a strong man's body pulsing close to mine. I turned away, went to my parlour immediately, not pausing even to watch him watch her as she tripped daintily, chastely, up the wide stairway.

The passionate force which erupted in me took me by surprise. I had thought my days of passion long since past. But in the instant when I spied on their greedy desire, Rowland's hands were upon my breasts again, and I yearned for him just as strongly as I had at fifteen years old. Never once had I felt that longing, through all my empty married years. In my widowhood I had thought such things were finished with. Yet, as I played over in my mind the master of Thornfield's longing for possession of the governess's body, and tasted what she felt – his lips kissing hers, his arms circling her, his manhood thrusting for her, I yearned so deeply for some satisfaction that I cried out aloud and grasped my hands together till the joints cracked, to stop myself from pressing down and down among my skirts to touch and bring relief.

The moment passed, the fire dying down as quickly as it had arisen, and I was myself again. The practicalities and unique problems of the situation absorbed me. What should I say to her in the morning? What should I say or do to warn her, to put her on her guard?

And what in all conscience could I say, without hypocrisy or dishonour? My own history, hidden away though it has been, was commonplace enough, but years ago I had given him my word, when he traded his secret for mine and bound my loyalty and silence so inextricably to him.

And so, as always, I would have to continue to play the respectable, deferential dame, speaking half truths and evasions and disregarded platitudes.

12

PARLOUR

I am sitting in my parlour unable – or unwilling – to fix myself to any household tasks. Today John is burning swept up leaves in the orchard and the smoke drifts past the window in a sweet smelling grey cloud. I have my Bible before me open at today's lesson, as has been my wont, though truth to tell my attention has always strayed from that daily exercise. However, it has suited my station and has aligned me with the expectations of others that I should be so employed for a quarter of an hour after breakfast each morning.

It was just so on last Midsummer morning. I had slept fitfully, I remember, and had woken weary, chasing thoughts of the past and the future round my head. Most likely, it seemed to me, her reproving hand would be raised so firmly and so often that, angered and humiliated beyond tolerance, Mr. Rochester would forsake Thornfield and find his pleasure elsewhere. Alternatively, she might, with righteous self-sacrifice, remove herself from temptation and insist on finding another situation. Giving herself heart, soul and body without a wedding ring on her finger she would not do. And marriage I knew to be impossible. There was nothing for it but to bide my time and wait for what should occur between the governess and my master. So I was sitting, as always, spectacles on nose and Bible open before me, when Mr. Rochester knocked once, entered and spoke six words to me.

'I am to marry Miss Eyre,' he said and turned to stride straight out.

This I had not expected and he must have seen the surprise, the contradictions, on my face even before I breathed a coherent word.

He paused. 'No dispute. No discourse. It will be as I say. And within this month. Continue to guard your respectable tongue, Mrs. Fairfax.' He fixed me with his dark, flashing eye and was gone.

And so when she tripped in some few minutes later I had no difficulty in acting out my astonishment. I called on all the resources of conventionality to remind her of the Rochesters' perennial avarice, and to advise her to tread carefully. I touched on the wide difference in their years, and in their station, on her insularity and ignorance and his knowledge of the wider ways of the world, concluding with the caution that gentlemen in his walk of life do not commonly marry their governesses.

Crestfallen at my admonishments and reservations she may have been, but at the sound of his voice calling to her from the hallway to hurry and join him, she cast me one quick, glittering glance and with barely a courtesy turned to speak to Adele, who ran in with a request to go with the couple to Millcote.

And I was left with only my whirling thoughts for company.

What could I say or do? Knowing with certainty the truth of the rumours relating to the inhabitant of the third storey should I not, in all conscience, breathe a word or pen a note to inform the governess of the existence of a supreme impediment to her marriage? If I did so she would demand proof, which could easily be given. But revealing that proof would very likely bring ignominy, shame and ruin on the man she clearly adored and who, it was crystal clear, doted on her to such an extent that he was willing to risk even the horror of exposure for her love.

For my own part, his threat or warning made little impression on me. There was not much for me to lose. True, my name and respectability were precious to me but they were nothing in comparison to the passionate love I had glimpsed the evening before. And, more than that, I too had felt such love. As a girl, younger even than the governess, I had relished its heady intoxication and revelled in its consummation. Remembering that, it seemed to me that considerations of respectability were as worthless and flimsy as the ash, blowing from an autumn bonfire.

13

THE STAIRCASE

I have almost given up hope of hearing word of our master's return. I continue to fill my days with household duties, finding occupation for my hands while my mind runs where it will. I have paused on the wide oak staircase just beneath the portrait of Edward Middleton Rochester, the present master's grandfather. The family resemblance is plain in the broad forehead and in a certain wildness in the dark eyes. I never knew him, of course, saw him only once when I was just a very little child – a shambling stooping wreck of a man with shaking hand and dribbling mouth; his appearance repulsed me, I recall.

I am carrying a jar of our best beeswax and three good, thick dusters. I woke this morning to a cold, bright day. Sunlight poured through the wide mullioned east window over the turn of the central staircase, and I noticed that stairs and rails and banisters were coated in a thick sheath of dust. So, with dusters and beeswax I have set about putting all to rights. Leah told me such cleaning and polishing were her duty but I have found her other work to do, happy to be left with my self-imposed task – and my thoughts.

I started at the top of the staircase and worked my way down, dusting, cleaning corners, removing every spider and web, till no speck of dirt remained. Then I climbed up again, armed with the sweet-smelling beeswax, and slowly, meticulously, began to make my way downwards yet again, step by step.

The staircase of Thornfield Hall is massy, built of stout oak nigh on three centuries ago, with shallow steps, their treads worn in gentle undulations by generations of Rochester feet. The uprights of the banisters are intricately carved, embossed with shields bearing traces of various ciphers. Standing out clearest of all of these are rooks – birds and turrets both – emblematic of the woodlands which abound the Rochester lands and the crenellations of the Hall itself.

Stooping to do the preliminary dusting, kneeling to rub in the beeswax, and then the final polishing until the oak gleams and glows – I find all this tiring work at my time of life. And time consuming too! Almost all the daylight hours have passed while I have been at my work. I watch my hands, spotted with one or two liver-coloured marks of ageing, and know that it is not only because I am house-proud that I have reserved this task for myself. No, in truth, as I kneel on each step and my hands caress the woodwork, it is almost as if I am praying, or as if I am paying homage to this, the very spine of Thornfield Hall, the family home of the unloving man whom I have always loved.

My duster scoops the beeswax from the jar – not too thickly – and slides along the tread, left to right, then back along the riser, right to left, snuggles into the corners. It takes skill to feed the crevices of the wood just so, and to glaze lightly each facet of the carvings. The banister itself will be so easy. Smooth, flat. I will leave that for the finish.

Now and then I pause. My arm is aching. My back is tired but I will not leave the task half done. What if Mr. Rochester were to return, today, this very evening, and find the staircase glassy with wet polish? I tell myself to keep working, not to let myself slacken in my endeavour.

Once or twice I see Leah watching me as she passes through

the hall below or along the passageway above, busy on some pretext or other. She may have spoken to me but I have not heard her. She shakes her head but I disregard her and continue with my work. It is strangely soothing, this mundane task, and I have to keep my mind on what I am doing if, when all is completed, I am to be satisfied, am to approve of my efforts.

I allow myself one indulgence. At the start of work on every step I pause. I rest my weary arm a little, drop my duster and look upwards. All along the staircase wall, stepped like the stairs themselves, hang portraits. Whether large or small, each is finely framed in gilt, and each takes its part in chronicling the history of Thornfield Hall and its masters. Damer de Rochester, in rusty armour, gazes sternly down from his place above the topmost stair and next after him is James Edward, embellished in curled wig and pointed collar of delicate lace. The others follow in their changing fashions of waistcoats and whiskers, draperies, neckties and jackets, until the well-known face of Frederick Rowland looks down at me, the avaricious cast of his eye seeming to search into the shadows of the entrance hall. His face is the final one in this pageant of Rochester lineage. Next after him should hang an artist's representation of his elder son, his heir, Rowland, my wilful, wicked Rowland, but that he did not live to inherit Thornfield Hall, dying in that accident in Biarritz even while his father lay on his own fatal sick-bed.

So now even Rowland's painted eyes do not gaze down at me any more than his physical eyes would have done were he here today. I was little more than a child when I had to learn that lesson. But it was a hard lesson to learn and I have often fallen into the fault of dreaming, hoping, imagining that he would have glanced at me once again. It matters not that he abandoned me in my time of trouble. His brother kept his maniac wife beneath this very roof, might easily have incarcerated her elsewhere – perhaps at Ferndean (ah! Ferndean!) – but he kept her near. I hold to the notion that Rochester men stay loyal, repeatedly beat my mind with that thought, though my experience and my torture tell me otherwise.

The long case clock in the hallway strikes the half hour. How long have I stood here, my eyes pinned to the blankness of the wall where a portrait should be, and wondering if the present Edward Rochester's likeness will ever hang there? I hear there is a rector's young son, over Halifax way, who is making a name for himself as a portrait painter. He might make a good job of it. But Mr. Edward has never, until this last year, remained here long enough to commission such a thing.

Suddenly I notice that the sunlight is gone. The staircase is shadowy, the eyes of the portraits peering through the gloom as if they are searching for something, for someone. A coolness steals through the air and for a moment, in a way I cannot fathom, I feel with a certainty that is beyond question, that no new portrait will ever be hung beside the great stairway at Thornfield Hall.

Shivering, I stoop to pick up my duster. I glance around. Has anyone seen me transfixed here? Leah? John? Grace Poole? All is quiet in this sombre autumn afternoon. Perhaps I have not been observed.

Briskly I recommence my polishing, faster and faster as the daylight thickens and the shadows deepen. Leah comes to me, suggests that she helps me complete the work, but I reject her offer and instruct her instead to bring a lamp and hold it steady for me till my work is done.

***

The clock struck eight before my work was finished. I had just sent Leah off to return the dusters and beeswax to the store cupboard when I saw Mrs. Poole on her way aloft with her pint of porter and her pudding. She is habitually taciturn so I was surprised when she stopped me to say that she thought her patient had made middling progress since 'that governess' had gone. Rarely fractious these days, Mrs. Rochester has enjoyed longer periods of calm and has sat, by the hour, brushing her mane of hair. Today she had asked for pen and paper and attempted to write a letter to her husband. However, beyond foul language and filth, Grace doubted there would be much sense in it.

Nodding a goodnight which concluded our conversation before I could frame a reply, she handed me a sheet of paper and continued upstairs. The letter was not sealed. Presumably, remembering some distressing former incidents, Mrs. Poole does not allow her patient access to tinder or open flame.

14

LIBRARY

I have placed the letter on my master's desk.

So, here it sits in this shadowy, silent room, holding within its white sheet – what?

An accusation? A curse? Who knows?

For a moment I think of opening its folds and reading what is written there. I do not examine my motives but I feel a sharp curiosity to know what she can have to say to him, and so I stand for a long minute with my hand outstretched, considering.

Then, resolute, I move away and leave the room. I close the library door firmly and turn the key in the lock, fortifying myself in that way to resist the temptation.

15

ENTRANCE HALL

I have lost count of how long Mr. Rochester has been away, searching for Jane Eyre, but it appears that his search has been fruitless, for this afternoon I received a hasty note from him telling me that he will return to Thornfield Hall tomorrow – alone.

I have his scrawled and blotted message in my hand even now, headed The White Hart Inn at Raskelf, a place I reckon to be some twenty-five miles off. He will have a long ride in the morning, for he is to meet with his lawyer in Millcote tomorrow afternoon before returning here, as he hopes, before nightfall.

So I bustle about seeing that his chamber and bed clothes are well aired and that fires are lit in the major rooms downstairs. I know how gloomy he has always thought the Hall to be with its panelled walls and shadowy passageways within, its grey stonework, and rookery and thorn bushes without. And with its dark, one-time secret. Perhaps some roaring log fires will cheer him when he returns. His spirits will be sore in need of cheering.

Busy with my household tasks, preparing for his return, I feel less troubled than for many a day. While I have checked the kitchen stores with Cook and supervised Leah's cleaning duties my thoughts have fixed on such commonplace activities, and the shades and wraiths which have whispered in my ears and passed before my eyes recently have seemed to retreat and cloak themselves, becoming well-nigh invisible. Almost free of their visitations, I feel a lightening of my spirits.

I notice Leah smiles with a look of relief to hear me giving clear instructions to John and requesting him to fetch more logs and coals from the fuel store in the stable yard. He nods and goes about his business. When the kitchen door has closed behind him I think I should ask him to take a coal bucket and a replenished log basket straight upstairs to Mr. Edward's room, to save Leah the drudgery of lugging them up the steep back staircase.

Going into the hall to don my cloak, I hear a half-stifled, wailing sound. The wind has risen and found its way underneath the Hall's ancient doorway. The fringe of the Turkey carpet trembles and shivers like some small animal. A window latch rattles.

I wrap my cloak tightly around me and let myself out, following John's path into the kitchen yard. It is cold, with a damp chill that sets my bones aching within seconds. I see the dense bushes in the laurel walk buffeted by the wind. It is a north-easterly which has arisen and blows strongly across the parkland, bringing with it, I shouldn't wonder, a sharp early snowfall. Mr. Edward will have a hard journey of it tomorrow.

But I am gratified to think that the newly lit fires are drawing well and that, with each gust of the wind, no smoke has yet billowed down any chimney to make eyes smart or to settle a covering of dust onto the furniture. Jack Dyer has done his work satisfactorily.

I see John and pass on my instructions to him. As he sets off towards the hall with the first of his loads I turn away and within less than a minute find myself at the archway of the stable yard. I know, immediately, that I should have stayed within the house busying my mind with practicalities. But I am here, now, where I have not stood for many a long day, in the place I have shunned instinctively because of its associations.

...The sound of distant hoof beats carries on the driving wind and a fifteen-years girl, a sun bonnet tied on her brown curls, is waiting in the autumn evening, cheeks flushed, heart racing, hoping that he will come to her, as she has waited and hoped in Hay Lane, as she has written and asked, *begged* that he should.

The hooves thud closer and closer. The girl raises her head expectantly. She scans the lane and driveway for a first glimpse of the adored figure, hatless, his dark hair tied back, his brown leather boots thrust deep into the stirrups, his body moving as one with the motion of his horse. There, there in a swirl of dust, the figures approach.

Nearer ... nearer...

But something is amiss. There is a distortion in what she sees, what she hears. The hoof beats are too rapid, the animal's stride too short for the thoroughbred Sultan, the rider too slight to be Rowland. This is some boy on a fell pony.

Once again the girl knows he has not come to her. She turns quickly away, trying to hide herself behind the alder bushes which flourish near the stable gateway. But he has seen her, the rider, and drawing rein, calls out to her as he dismounts and walks towards where she shrinks away.

'Alice,' he says. 'Alice Redmond. You're waiting, as he said you would.'

She had been about to edge away, avoiding any conversation, but at his final words she finds herself walking towards him. With a conscious effort she holds her head high. Perhaps there is some message, some reason for his absence, something his brother can explain. She waits, heart beating, breathless, attempting composure, but hoping, hoping, waiting for what the boy will say.

He begins to speak. 'He told me to tell you—' but as he looks at her wide, troubled eyes, at her slight frame, at her thin-fingered hand trembling slightly as it rests at her waist, he stops. There is a redness washing over his open face. He swallows, noisily, tries to speak, clears his throat which is suddenly dry. After a moment he takes a breath and tries once more.

'You cannot have known,' he begins and falters again. 'Did he not tell you he was going away?'

She shakes her head. She cannot speak. There is too much to understand.

'Yes – going away – for quite some time.' He glances at her. She is rock still now. 'To, to London first, and after that to Boulogne and then— ' He cannot catalogue the cities she will only have heard others mention; she will not know where they are. 'Oh, then to a number of other places. On our father's business,' he adds, as if that makes all clear.

She is not certain that she has asked the question aloud but she must have done, for he answers her. 'For upwards of a year, I believe. Perhaps by next midsummer he will be here again—'

And it is then that the tears overwhelm her and she sobs and cries and it looks to the boy as if she would fall down there in the dust of the track under the arched gateway of the stable yard...

I am surprised to find that it is almost dark when I re-enter the Hall. Mrs. Poole passes me carrying her tray with its usual covered dish and mug of porter. She nods once, when I tell her that the master will return tomorrow but she pauses only long enough to ask how long he will remain. She continues on her way aloft to her charge, however, without waiting for a reply.

And, in truth, I could not have given her an answer. Edward Fairfax Rochester's activities and decisions have puzzled me ever since he grew to be a man and inherited Thornfield Hall with all its riches and its responsibilities. Though, God knows, I understood him well enough when he was a child.

True, he is known by all folk locally as a man of gloomy moods, a man whose brooding fury is barely suppressed beneath his harsh countenance. True, there have been countless rumours of abandoned mistresses and continental dalliance and base-born child or children. What though he is now accused of bigamy, and has sought to ruin the governess by an illegal marriage? And deceived her cruelly, too? I cannot bring myself to condemn him. For I have cause to know and to remember that before his stay in the West Indies, which changed him beyond recall, and before he inherited Thornfield Hall, which I have heard him call the curse upon his life, he was a man good at heart.

When he was but a youth, with a grown man's understanding, how kindly and compassionate he was! His goodness to me at that time over-rides all else for me. And he has kept faith for nigh on a quarter of a century, never breathing a word of my secret shame. And for those immeasurable kindnesses I am bound in his service for ever.

16

BEDCHAMBER

It was late when I retired to bed and I expected to fall asleep within minutes, tired as I am after the busy-ness of the day and the wearisome pain of the stable-yard visitation. But as I lie here listening to the gale which still blows about the house, I count the quarter hours as they pass, marked by the chimes of St Saviour's clock. The wind veers and fluctuates and the bells echo faintly at times as if from a great distance, then clang so sonorously that one might think the church tower stood as close as the laurel walk.

Half past two, a quarter to three, three o'clock, a quarter past.

It is no good. I cannot sleep, yet, weary as I am, I lack the strength to rouse myself fully and strike the tinder to light the candle by my bedside.

For a moment the wind drops and there is silence. Then, as if it had merely drawn breath, it starts again with a sudden rattling gust. It is as startling as gunshot, or as pebbles thrown against the window pane. A hailstorm is breaking and the buffeting wind blows harder than ever, its wailing voice circling the hall like some doomed fairy-tale creature begging for admission. Winter has come early this year.

Of all weathers, a wild wind troubles me most. The fretful turbulence tears my spirits, runs me ragged with its unpredictability, tires me. Even as a child I remember my mother's reprimands when, while a gale blew, I could not abide to sit with my knitting or my sampler work, or even settle myself with a book though I dearly loved reading and my parents always encouraged that interest. Instead I would pace through the farmhouse, hang about the doorways, watch at windows, thinking that the trees would snap their trunks as they bent and creaked at the mercy of the wind. One time, not long before her death, Mother so far lost patience with my restlessness that she raised her hand to me – swollen and bloated with the dropsy as it was – and caught me a stinging blow which left my ear ringing louder than the wind itself. How old was I then? Eight? Nine years old? 'Tis over forty years ago, in truth, that wild windy night.

And a fierce, dry wind blew on the night I went away.

I have little recollection of the time between my meeting with Ted in the stable yard and the evening when I left the village of Hay, for ever, as I assumed. There was a cloudiness in my thoughts and a suffocating heaviness around me, a feeling of complete helplessness. I could make no sense of my world, my life or my future, formulate no plan, understand no means of escape from what was to come. Even my body was out of my control. I had always been slight and lithe and now, daily it seemed to me, my shape thickened and a torpor drank at my vitality. I remember my father's troubled look one evening as he watched me strain to lift a pitcher of milk in the dairy. He said no word and neither did I, but his eyes questioned and I think he knew.

Ted had told me to wait. Had said little more than that he understood the reason for my tears and shame. I could not think he had any influence over his elder brother but there was no one else in whom I could put my trust and so, in a limbo-like existence, I did as he bid. Returned to the farm; went about my daily business; waited.

It was a surprise when Rowland's father visited our farm one day in October. Usually any estate business was transacted through Mr. Rochester's land agent. He did not dismount from his horse, would not enter our house, but came straight out with his proposition. The elderly lady who had been nanny to Mr. Rowland and Mr. Edward had been retired to a property some distance away, owned by the Rochester family, Ferndean Manor. Mrs. Howard's health was deteriorating and she was in need of a housemaid and companion. Would Alice Elizabeth take the position? He wanted an immediate answer.

I do not know what it cost my father to agree. In view of what happened to him a few months later, I think perhaps his mind preyed on the decision he made there and then. When I nodded my acceptance of Mr. Rochester's proposition, Father was quick to make his thanks and voice his approval. And after it was agreed, he never talked of my return or the duration of my service at Ferndean. I imagine, his unspoken suspicions being what they were, that he regarded the proposal as a blessing for us both.

I know that, having once begun to retrace the pattern of my life in this way, I shall have no rest tonight. I light my candle and, cold as it is, get out of bed and walk across to the window. Moonlight flickers as the clouds billow across the sky like flimsy curtains. And, yes, small scattered flakes of snow are starting to fall.

I return to my bed before my feet have chilled too much and, whether I wish it or no, the pictures of the past float before my eyes.

Ferndean! Remote, enclosed by woodland as it is, the Manor House provided a safe and welcome hiding place for me, a kind of hibernation in the months that followed. But what a place it is! Resting in a hollow, its situation is not salubrious and it is separated from the dense woodland which runs almost up to the doorway by only a scant plot of rough turf land. I know not if the Rochesters thought well of Mrs. Howard, but I suspect that the landlord had acquired a housekeeper for the old place at very little expense to himself when he pensioned that old lady off to live there. And she in turn had in me the services of a maid of all work and a nurse in return for the pittance I was paid.

During the winter, while my baby grew within me and the old lady wasted away beside me, there were times when I thought that none of us would survive until the spring. The cold, dank dampness of the house fostered foul smelling moulds which grew black like coal dust or grey like dandelion clocks on the flagstones of the hallway and the bedrock of the cellars and beneath the stairs. Through November and December I was plagued with a wracking cough and head cold and, when the new year turned, my nose ran and my bones ached in a way I had never known, and which has left a tenacious legacy. I aged a year for every month that I was there, I believe, and knew not how I should fare when my time came.

To say that I was lonely at Ferndean would be an understatement. Apart from the dying old lady, the only other folk I saw during those dark winter months were an occasional pedlar or gipsy who knocked at the door, and from time to time a visit from the wife of the estate woodman, who was our nearest neighbour dwelling a half mile away.

It was Mrs. Haxby who sent word to Thornfield when I feared that old Mrs. Howard was nearing her end, but there was no reply by the time the old lady breathed her last on that January night. Alone, I pressed her eyelids closed and unlatched the window to release her spirit into the wintry darkness. Alone, I looked at the parchment skin of her face, the bones jutting at her jaw, her splintered teeth and her dry mouth open, fixed, immobile. I sat and held her hand while it chilled and clenched rigid in my grasp, and my candle flame guttered and flickered beside me. My skirt was stretched tight across my stomach and I saw the movements of the unborn child, felt its flexings in my womb. How strange it all was – the aged dame whose life had finished, the unborn child alive within me and I, there, between the two, held by, holding them both.

It was the next morning that Young Mr. Edward – as in the last few months he had grown to be – arrived. He had asked to come in his father's stead and Mr. Frederick was easily persuaded to let his son deputise. There was business to be transacted in Malton and the death of an old retainer was not something a busy man could trouble himself with when there were important deals to be done. So the necessary arrangements were made by the young man and he stayed at Ferndean for two nights until the funeral and interment ceremonies were completed.

Only after the funeral did I venture to ask Mr. Edward what should become of me now that there was no old lady to tend. He was standing at the doorway, ready to fetch his horse from the rough stall where it was housed and set off on his return journey. For a moment he paused, seeming to search for words. He had represented his father at Ferndean during the last two days and dealt competently with affairs on the estate there, but I reminded myself that despite his manly physique he was still but a youth. If he was embarrassed by my condition he hid it well; I noticed only that he never let his eyes rest on my stomach. He looked me in the eye as I waited, fearing his answer, for if I were to be turned out I did not know where I should go. But he told me that I should remain at Ferndean until Easter, and it was then that I ventured to mention his brother.

'Still abroad,' he stated and turned his eyes away from me. It was clear that Rowland admitted no responsibility for me and if old Mr. Rochester had any compunction regarding the fate of his tenant farmer's child, he probably reckoned that providing food and lodgings for a six-month was benevolence beyond any call of duty.

'There is one thing I should tell you,' he said, once again looking at me directly with those strong, dark eyes. 'I had thought to keep it from you but I do not like deceptions – unless they are unavoidable.' He paused, drew breath and then spoke rapidly. 'It is about your father. He has not been in good health over the winter. His mind has been troubled, his sleep disturbed, he said. But he has worked as hard as ever. Until recently, that is.'

I held my breath. He paused again. Began again. 'He suffered a seizure nigh on a week ago and his recovery is – slow, I fear.'

I felt the tears sting my eyes even before he had finished speaking. Father! My dearly loved father! I saw his face before me, his kind eyes, his weatherbeaten skin, the greying tufts of his whiskers.

Mr. Edward raised a hand and patted my shoulder clumsily. 'Miss Redmore, Alice,' he said. 'Try not to fret. It cannot be good for you – at this time. I trust, I hope, your father will continue to improve.' He stopped again, and I forced myself to quieten my sobbing. 'Dr Whittle has attended him.' Yet another pause. 'He has not quite given up hope of some further recovery.'

It was bad, then. And I did not need to be told what that meant. If my father was permanently incapacitated by the seizure, if he could not live a vigorous, active life and manage the farm, he would lose livelihood and home and hearth at one and the same time. Mr. Edward's father would not risk the profitability of Hall Farm for the sake of compassion or consideration of its tenant.

Within five minutes Mr. Edward had fetched his horse and ridden away. There was nothing else he could say or do to aid me and he was required back at Thornfield. He held my hand briefly and wished me well, hoping that my 'remaining weeks at Fearndean' as he put it, would be tranquil. He put two sovereigns into my hand as recompense, he said, for my final ministrations to Mrs. Howard, but it was a gross overpayment and I believe I have his generosity to thank for the money. And then he was gone and the dank woodlands seemed to advance towards me and close in around me, even as the sound of the hoofbeats faded in the distance.

If I had been lonely before Mrs. Howard's death, the last three months of my pregnancy were even more desolate. The old lady had not been well enough to be a companion to me, but her presence in the gloomy old house, and her needs, had provided purpose and pattern in my otherwise aimless life. After she was gone the drab months of January, February and March passed, their days indistinguishable to me, wrapped in a prolonged season of wetness and fogs. The old nurse's funeral was the last service I attended at St Bartholomew's Church, for I could not abide the glances and whispers from the straight-faced, narrow little community that worshipped there. And so Sunday was no different from weekday and the slow months slid by in a grey anonymity.

I did not count the days of my allotted time, took no heed of the signs my body gave me. I do not know what would have happened if Mrs. Haxby had not chanced upon me that particular evening, finding me bent double, panting, a fierce, sharp, tearing pain splitting me in two, and the child almost born there in the mud and rot of the kitchen garden.

She was a good, honest woman, Eliza Haxby. Her aid was immediate and adept and her advice, following the birth of my red, wrinkled daughter, sound and sensible.

And I did not want to hear it.

She left me with my thoughts through that long night.

I did not sleep. As now, I counted the quarter hours notched through the night by the church clock. I held my child tight in my arms, marvelling at her fashioning, her plump cheeks, the skin as soft as a July apricot, the delicacy of her eyelash threads. I sat there, trying to pretend that the embrace with which I greeted my daughter was not, in reality, a goodbye; my welcome not a farewell.

For Eliza's words were sound and sensible, like herself. Keep my daughter with me and I'd be called a trollop. Keep her with me and she, sinless as she was, would be branded bastard. Let her go.

But where? I had blocked off every thought of this event, this day. I was not ready. And I did not want to loose her from my arms. I thought that I had known love during the last summer; but in that April night I believe I learnt love's meaning for the first time in my life.

Daylight brought decision. I knew that I would have to let my daughter go. Abandon her? Release her.

When she came I had all ready. Numb beyond tears, I handed her the two wrapped bundles: in one the garments I had stitched, each with its simple embroidery of a daisy; in the other, the child I had carried. Some miles off Mrs. Haxby had a grieving cousin whose baby, born too early, had let go of life even as it began, just days ago. It was providence, she said.

In my heart I named my daughter Dorothea, gift from God, and I gave my gift away as the sun rose and daylight stretched across the gravel walk and through the woodland.

And it is almost daylight, now.

I sit by the window, wrapped in a blanket, and see there is a slackening of the darkness over the rookery. Though I have not slept I must wash and dress and busy myself. I find my spirits lift a little at the thought that in a few hours the master will be home. I will do all that I can to soften his solitary return. It will not be easy for him.

17

LIBRARY

All morning, while I should have been attending to the preparations for Mr. Rochester's return, my mind has drifted away from my tasks and I have watched another homecoming played out like a dream before my tired eyes.

The visitations began early. Before breakfast I went out to gather some Michaelmas daisies to dress the hallway. I have always liked to see the purple blooms set against the oaken panelling. As I looked down towards the rookery, my arms full of the tall flowers, I saw, quite clearly, a grey-cloaked figure disappearing into the woodland. She was carrying something tenderly in her arms, and had a bundle of clothes or some such dangling from her wrist. Eliza Haxby!

In an instant I was trembling, faint, and felt again that gaping, hollow emptiness which I thought the years had blotted out.

I turned and walked back slowly toward the Hall, its setting and its form familiar, reassuring. And then, out of nowhere, a desolate little figure, slumped, dizzy, on a single step before the narrow door of a dank manor house.

I rubbed my eyes, shook the wraith away and re-entered Thornfield Hall. But once inside, the past surged up to meet me and, like sunlight working on a piece of glass in tinder, a spark of longing flickered in my dry heart. I relived the need that I had felt that day when I was left doubly alone, the need to return to the place where I had been cherished, loved. If I did not return to the farm, if I remained solitary and unloved, that longing would eat away at my very identity, would perhaps destroy me.

I left Betsey, John, Leah, Grace, all of them, to attend to their allotted duties and hid myself away from them here in the master's library, under the pretence of dusting the bookshelves. But I have done no work. Instead I have sat near the fireside and let the visiting figures act out their tableaux of the past as they wished.

> ...A young woman, moving mechanically, gathers some belongings and ties them up in a clumsy parcel. She takes bread and water. She dons bonnet and cloak. The iron key grates in the door of the gloomy house and is placed under a stone. A figure walks, never once looking behind her, into the woodland and away...

Midway on my homeward journey I rested at an inn, I remember, blessing Mr. Edward for the coins he had given me which amply funded my lodging that night and a place on a carrier's cart the next morning. It was midday when I saw the familiar landscape of Hay, got down from the cart, and began to walk the last half mile to the farmhouse.

There it was. How warm its creeper-clad walls looked in the spring afternoon sunlight. How fine the fields were, stretching away down the shallow incline to the south. What a contrast to the dark shadows of Ferndean forest, where the trees had seemed to stretch forward to encircle and grasp that old house, and draw all breath from anyone within its walls.

…And standing by the gate, she sees him – an old man, walking slowly and with unsteady tread across the stack yard. He stoops, bowing his head to his stride, his left foot never fully raised, the toe of his muddy boot dragging across the packed earth with a rasping sound. Her father. What a longing she feels to lean against him, to see him smile at her.

She hastens forward, her eyes suddenly filled with tears. Since her delivery, through decision and through separation, she has watched and moved dry-eyed. Now, seeing the ruin that was once her father, the tears fall. As if all the fluids of her body are in flood, she feels the blood, hot and thick between her legs, feels a tingling strain in her swollen breasts and a wetness oozing from her nipples as the milk comes in, staining the flowers on her cotton bodice with its stickiness.

She draws her shawl tighter across her body, hoping he cannot see the tell-tale wetness as he lifts his one strong arm to hold and welcome her.

There is pain in his eyes, and questioning and doubt. But they do not speak of these things, merely hold one another in a long embrace until suddenly, no matter how weary she may be, he must lean on her and she feels his weight dragging down upon her shoulder and she guides him into their home…

Perhaps I have slept for a while. Suddenly I hear Leah and Betsey talking loudly in the hall. I quit the Library to ask them what they are about. Has he returned? Is all ready?

Both begin to answer me and at first I can make neither head nor tail of it. Then, as Leah takes over the story, it becomes clear. John has just brought news that their master's return is to be delayed. It seems he has heard tell of some gentlewoman seeking shelter at the Union House in a manufacturing town a day's ride west of Millcote. He has convinced himself that this must be Miss Eyre and has ridden thence, deferring his return until he can bring the young woman back with him.

Well, we shall see. It passes me how he can persuade himself first that this is she, and then that she will obey his wish. How it will answer I cannot tell. All I know is that I feel a burning annoyance at this delay and, not for the first time, I wish that Mr. Rochester had never clapped eyes on this meddlesome governess.

I carry my emptiness back into the Library with me. I had been hoping that when he returned he would be his old, moody troubled self, a morose employer in all conscience, but one I knew and understood. One I cared for and served loyally. A firm man of some dignity. Not this husk of what he was.

Was I doomed under some curse, I wonder, to watch all the men I loved crumble or demean themselves, until only pitiful weakness or shamefulness remain where all had once been so fine and admirable?

The last time I saw Rowland flashes before my eyes with stark clarity. He was drunk, of course, stumbling out of the Rochester Arms and shambling towards the stable yard. He did not see me. I had wanted to approach him, married woman though I now was, pointless though I knew it would be. But I hung back, my eyes caressing the curve of his chin, the span of his wrist, the length of his thigh. He paused, rocking a little on his unsteady legs and braced himself to draw a flask from his pocket, tilting his head back to swig its contents. Then stopped. Listening. And I heard low humming from somewhere in the yard and saw Joan, the landlord's wife, leaning against the stable door, unthreading the ribbon of her bodice. From deep in his chest he made a throaty, laughing sound which I knew so well, and set off, striding clumsily across the yard until he flung himself at her and they tumbled together into the darkness of the stable.

My father stumbled too, though it was not drink which

unmanned him. He was ill when I returned to Hall Farm, wearing out his stricken body and troubled mind in his brave attempt to keep at his daily work. We were together less than a week before a second seizure, much more violent than the first, felled him. I ran from the kitchen, saw his twisted, twitching body and knelt beside him while he tried to speak, his thoughts trapped in the clicking of throat and tongue and teeth. He died before I could catch a word.

And so I knelt beside him on the solid flag-stoned floor in a turning formless world, a parentless daughter, a wife with no husband, a mother with no child.

18

PARLOUR

Although All Hallows Day is only just passed, Thornfield is gripped in a spell of fiercely cold weather, the ground iron-hard, and the dusting of snow which fell two nights ago frozen sharp and rigid. When I woke this morning I saw clouds like weighty grey bolsters rolling in from the west and knew that the dry spell was over and we would be in for a heavy snow storm. Would Mr. Rochester return today?

By mid-morning I had word from him. Jem Mudge of the Rochester Arms had gone to Wetherby market yesterday. There he chanced upon the master drinking not ale but spirits, he said with a knowing look, at the White Hart Inn. He handed over a short letter, adding that he hardly recognised Mr. Edward. He has aged ten years in recent weeks, it seems.

While I was talking to the young man, Leah came out into the yard, wearing the mauve dress which suits her colouring so well. She was shaking crumbs from a tablecloth that looked perfectly clean to me. Jem coloured up when he saw her and stood, the breath rising from his slightly parted lips like wisps of smoke, watching as she stretched her arms up high. He would have wanted to stay and talk to her, I'll be bound, but snow was starting to fall and so I thanked him for bringing the letter and told him to hasten back to Hay before a blizzard set in.

Back in my parlour I read the missive.

She is nowhere to be found,

he has written, the words scrawled hastily, the lines sloping away down the page.

*I am weary with searching. There is nothing for it but to return to Thornfield its accursed walls doubly hateful to me now, housing the **wife** who is abhorrent to me – empty of the would-be wife I yearn for with a hopeless longing which—*

I broke off from reading, shocked that he could so reveal his loss and grief to me. What must be his state of mind that he should write thus to his housekeeper? Glossing over a couple more lines of heart-broken effusions, I noted the single, carelessly worded instruction contained in missive.

Do what you think needful for my return. I care not.
E.F.R.

Never in all the years have I known him write like this. I remember his first letter to me, when Thornfield Hall was new to me as housekeeper. Old Mr. Rochester was not long dead and Mr. Edward was yet to come home from the Indies. Strange though his instructions were, they were carefully phrased and clear. His young heart must have been wracked with disappointment, yet at that time he revealed nothing of his pain or of the deception which had been played upon him by his father and his brother. Even when we spoke of those things, after his return and when the lady was safely stowed on the third storey, he was guarded, controlled. Dignified.

Leah has just told me that it is time for lunch and I have

asked her to bring me some cold meat and pickles and a glass of cordial on a tray. As she goes on her errand to the kitchen, I lift down my writing box from its place on the shelf in the alcove and draw out a thin sheaf of letters from the concealed drawer. While I eat my simple meal I look over the old papers, yellowing now with age and dryness.

Here is the one, the only one, I ever received from Lionel.

> *My Dear Miss Redmond,*
>
> *In the months since your father's death the care you have taken of your aunt, Mrs. Pollard, has been most charitable and exemplary.*
>
> *Now that she has joined her brother in their heavenly reward, I beg to ask if you will care for another who has need of your devotion, by becoming the wife of*
> *Lionel Fairfax.*

Not the most romantic of proposals, but one which I accepted with little hesitation. When I received it I pondered, briefly, on whether I should reveal my history to the good clergyman, but I decided to stay mute on that score.

What made me practise this deception? Practicalities, first and foremost. My father and my aunt being dead, I had no home. The little money left to me would not support me long for the future. I was too slight and weak for farming work, having not been in robust health since leaving Ferndean. And what had I to gain by revealing the truth of my past? Eliza Haxby had taught me clearly the dangers of such honesty.

But more than these considerations, it was some words which Edward Rochester spoke to me which influenced me most. It was on the day of my father's funeral. He came to the service, no other from the family attending. After the Reverend Fairfax had spoken the words of committal, the few villagers who had gathered out of respect to my father fell away and I was left at the graveside, with only the young man beside me. I did not sob but I could not stop the tears coursing down my cheeks. He did not speak for some minutes but his eyes were upon me and after a while he took my hands in his and held them firmly.

'Alice,' he said, 'you must look forward now. Only forward. The past is gone.' He paused. He might be giving words of condolence to anyone bereaved. 'Treasure the precious things you remember.' He stopped again. It seemed to me that whenever he spoke to me he only stated one thought at a time. 'Treasure them,' he repeated, 'but keep them to yourself. And, if you do that,' he added after another pause, 'there will be an element of choice and freedom in your future.'

He turned away, glancing at the clergyman, a cousin of his, who was standing, waiting, near a bent yew tree. I caught a look pass between them and, I believe, Mr. Edward nodded his head at him in a kind of complicity. And then he was gone.

I fold up Lionel's note and take out a longer letter, penned years later. I place it on the table and put today's letter beside it. The handwriting is the same, but how changed! The strokes which were penned yesterday are faint and flimsy compared with the firm, determined lines of the older epistle in which he had set out his orders and stipulations. Some phrases leap off the paper as I cast my eyes over it.

> *...Secure and secluded accommodation ... the upper storey provides sanctuary, asylum ... a foreign lady whose troubled past must not be inquired into ... periods of violence ... danger of harm ... discretion of the utmost importance ... engage, after discreet and diligent search, the services of a nurse ... experienced in the field of such care ... no idle talk or gossip ... most generous remuneration if total discretion, **secrecy**, can be assured...*

I remember my surprise when I received that letter, and my curiosity too, wanting to know more of who had need of such especial care and why Mr. Rochester was at pains to provide it.

I owed Mr. Edward a sincere debt of gratitude, remembering the aid he had given me when I was a young unmarried woman and believing that he might well have been instrumental in suggesting to the elderly vicar of Hay that he should take a young wife to comfort his old age; so, I suppressed the questions which sprang into my mind, and set about fulfilling my master's requests as best I could.

In my childhood I had heard tales of a deranged woman who was locked up in the attic of a house beside the river Ure, not far from a cathedral city. Her seducer was, so the story went, a respected lawyer who, tired of her favours, cast her off. The disappointed woman threatened to reveal his conduct publicly, so he shut her mouth and attempted to save his reputation by imprisoning her in the attic of his home where she remained many a year, driven mad by her lover's rejection and by the cruelty of her imprisonment. If I came to any conclusion about the intended resident of Thornfield Hall, I thought along those lines; I recognized only that my master, whilst requiring secrecy for his own name's sake, seemed to be doing all within his power to ensure that this lady should be well cared for and kept in safety and some comfort.

And what of that lady now? I see again that creature scrabbling on all fours in the shadows of the garret room where we all stood askance and the master introduced us to his wife! Before that day I had caught only the occasional glimpse of her during the last ten years, though I remember her arrival here well enough.

It was a snowy winter afternoon, much like this. I was alone at the Hall, save for the woman I had recently employed. Discreet enquiries had led me to hear of a suitable nurse at the Grimsby Retreat and, after correspondence and a brief meeting in the remote village of Caistor in North Lincolnshire, I had offered Grace Poole the post insisting, as instructed, that absolute discretion was required and that no gossip of any kind be tolerated. She told me she liked her own company better than others' and her phlegmatic manner and taciturnity impressed me as ideal qualities in the servant I was seeking.

I gave John and Mary leave for a two-day visit to their relatives in Millcote and dismissed the day servants early on the afternoon when I expected Mr. Rochester's return. The winds blew and the snow fell as I watched for the approach of the hired carriage which would bring the travellers on the last stage of their journey from Escrick. As the light failed and evening fell, I heard at last the sound of coach wheels and a pair of horses. I ran to the stairs on the second storey and called to Mrs. Poole to attend.

We stood at the great front door as the carriage approached. Even before the wheels had stopped turning Mr. Rochester let down the window and called out, asking if we were alone. Alighting, he closed the carriage door behind him, keeping hold of it with his gloved hand and I introduced Mrs. Poole. He looked at her long and hard in the light of the lamp I was holding, and she held his gaze, straight and firm. 'You'll do, Nurse,' he said. 'Your work commences now. Assist me.'

He turned back to the carriage and released the door, ordered the coachman to remain where he was for the present and let down the steps himself. He positioned Mrs. Poole on one side of the door and motioned to me to take up a similar place on the other, before re-entering the coach himself. For a moment there was total silence. Then one of the horses stamped a hoof and whickered down its nose, the noises magnifying in the frosty air.

Mrs. Poole and I held to our posts, icy though it was, and waited as instructed. Two minutes passed and we heard nothing but the master's low voice reiterating a request to take his arm, leave the carriage, take his arm.

Suddenly a commotion broke the quiet stillness. Muffled cries and remonstrance fought with a clattering and stamping of feet upon the carriage floor and, before we were fully aware what was happening, the master was falling backwards out of the carriage, only saving himself from landing upon us both by grabbing the framework of the carriage itself. He muttered a curse under his breath, thrust his hands inside the coach and dragged – there is no other word for it – dragged his companion out into the cold, night air.

She was cloaked in a dark velvet wrapper and I could not see her face, so shaded was she by its hood. But two bright, fierce eyes blazed out under the lamplight and a flaming swathe of ruffled crimson silk shone out, a scarf wound around the lady's neck. I was put in mind of some tall, exotic glass-house flower, its rich petals framing the dark calyx of the bloom and for a moment I could not take my eyes from her.

But the master's voice broke my reverie, harshly ordering me to lead the way, requiring Mrs. Poole to take one of the lady's arms whilst he held the other. 'Firmly, firmly, Nurse. You must use your strength,' he warned.

They followed me, two sets of footsteps crunching clearly over the snow, accompanied by a sliding, dragging sound and a whimpering or mewing as a kitten might make if it were locked accidentally in a dark cellar or cupboard.

'You may take down the luggage now, driver,' Mr. Rochester shouted over his shoulder. 'Place it all inside the door.' He turned to me, never pausing in the progress to the staircase. 'Pay him off, Mrs. Fairfax, and wait in my Library until I need you.'

19

LIBRARY

And I am waiting in his library again, even now, noting nothing but the regular ticking of the mantle clock above the welcoming fire which burns in the grate. I sit at the window with my eyes fixed on the farthest point of the driveway, eager for the first glimpse of my master's return.

There has been no let up in the snow. The wind has dropped and there are no swirling blasts, but the flakes fall dense, heavy, silent. I move only to add another log, as required, to the fire. Mr. Rochester will need warmth and comfort when he returns. Though I fear any words of welcome which I can say will do little to ease his sadness.

The third time I rise from my chair, my eye fixes on the folded square of paper, lying stark white on the desk. Mrs. Rochester's letter. Before I know what I am doing, I feel its smoothness in my fingers, have unfolded it and am scanning its words.

> *Remember, Husband, how I died so often in your love, happy at the moment of each death. But still I live.*
>
> *I asked you once to give me peace. It is quiet here*

– unless I laugh or weep – but peace is elsewhere. I learnt power at your lips. But it mazes me, your power, for the sun is cooled and the skies are changed now that you do not love me.

And so I weep. Coulibri and Granbois blazed beautiful. Where have you hidden the guava bushes and the mango trees and the sweet-smelling hibiscus? You have wrapped up happiness in a parcel and taken it away when I wasn't looking, as I feared you would. I think you hate me and my cries burn my throat. I search and strive and seek for what is lost and know you hate me. And I weep.

And I am alone. And so are you.

And so is she.

I have seen meetings far below me, on the terrace, in the orchard, and a parting, too, a slippered shadow one dim dawn in a glimmering yard.

However far you travel, you are alone. I travel nowhere beyond my nightly quests. In the cold greyness which is in me and around me and has become my being, there is none to warm the chill that aches where my heart once was.

You feel that too? That void?

I would melt it for you should you beg me.

Your wife whose name is lost

I do not know what I expected to find in the letter but its words disturb me in a way I had not imagined. Poor, poor lady! What a heart-deep cry of longing is here. And I feel it, know it, too.

I see an angry creature with matted hair, scrabbling in the shadows. I see yellow teeth reaching for my master's throat, and hear cursing and blaspheming. I have never entertained the possibility that there could be sweetness and sorrow – empty yearning – within that raving creature's heart.

I replace the paper where it should have lain undisturbed. If

I have sinned in reading what was meant solely for another's eyes, I am punished for it now, for a physical reaction follows swiftly on my thoughts and I run from the library, run to the wide front door, thrust it open and stand there hanging on to the door frame for support, trembling, gulping the cold, clean air into my lungs. After a while my biliousness passes and I am left weak, shivering. My unfocused eyes follow the drift of the snowflakes as they fall and fall and fall.

I hear a quiet cough behind me, and Leah is in the hall. She looks troubled. She asks me what I am doing there, letting the cold blow into the house on such an evening. It is almost as if she is reprimanding me. I tell her to mind her own business and order her to return to the kitchen to check that all is in preparation of her master's evening meal.

Once she has gone through the baize-covered inner door, I return to the library to continue my vigil at the window and, as so often when I am alone, the past steps up before me and will not be ignored.

> ...He looks haggard, weary. He sighs as I pour his wine and take it to him. He sits in his high-backed chair beside the fire. I am about to go to the kitchen to bring him supper on a tray when he rouses himself and orders me to sit, pointing to the second chair flanking the hearth. I do as bidden.
>
> There is a long pause.
>
> The clock's tick sounds louder with every second that passes. But for a sigh and his arm occasionally stretching to raise the glass to his lips, or refill it from the carafe, I would think that the master slept.
>
> He does not speak. I grow uncomfortable, wonder if he has forgotten that I am there. I am about to rise stealthily and edge from the room, leaving him to his solitary musings, when he

speaks.

'Widow Fairfax,' he addresses me. 'Sit here with me for a while, if you please. I would talk with you.'

I wait but he is silent. What can he have to say to me? I have done all that he required. But I know his ways and so I wait. He will speak again when he is ready to do so.

The fire crackles and a sudden shaft of sparks shoots upwards as the logs slip and re-settle in the grate.

'First, I owe you some thanks.' His voice breaks through the waiting quiet of the room. 'Mrs. Poole is admirably suited to her employment, I believe. You did well to find her for me.'

I start to say that anything I can do to serve him is — but he breaks in peremptorily. 'Enough. Now, I reiterate. Your discretion, your loyalty, your silence in all matters relating to the hiring of Mrs. Poole, and to her employment here, are of paramount importance.'

I nod. I give him my word. I will not break his trust.

'You will wonder about the traveller who now resides—' He breaks off, his face suddenly distorted by a harsh grimace. Another long moment passes and, calming himself with a visible effort, he resumes. 'I must tell you that no dishonour attaches to that – (a pause) – that lady.' There is contempt and harshness in his voice which he cannot conceal...

My thoughts snap away from the recollection of the secrets he divulged to me that night. I do not want to hear again the story of his time in the Indies, the shameful incidents of his married life. But whilst I can silence the catalogue of his disillusionment, I cannot skim away from the details which torment me most. No matter how I try to blot it out, the echo of his harsh, embittered voice is inside my head again, telling me the part his brother played in the deception which he and his father acted upon young Edward Fairfax Rochester.

'...It was Rowland who told me the lies and half truths...'

I hear his tirade, the torrent of words and accusations tumbling out, buffeting my ears...

'...Rowland led me on... Rowland made promises... Fond, trusting fool I believed the lies Rowland told, the dreams, the delights Rowland promised...'

I look at him fixedly and I see my sorrow reflected in his dark eyes and all I can hear is that name, repeated and reverberating in my poor, aching skull...

And it is beating again now, now, now, here, in this same room, just as it did all those years ago and, inside my swirling pain, I recall his steady voice, controlled once more...

...'Listen to me, Alice. Listen. It cannot be spoken of again.

Never again. There is but one other in the world who knows the truth of my torment, and he is far away. Him apart, you are sole guardian of my secret. Keep it safely, as you would a poison locked away, hidden, unseen, lest it bring some fatal harm upon a blameless child.'

I tell him that he may be assured that he can trust me but he does not hear me.

'I would have kept you in ignorance, but you have dealt with matters for me and tonight you have seen too much. So, at this moment, as the clock's hands move to midnight, I bind you with this knowledge.'

Whether it be as caress or caution I cannot say, but he takes both my small, dry hands and clasps them firmly in his grip.

'Remember, Alice,' he says, so quietly that I strain to hear him, as he leans forward in his chair, his broad curly head close to mine, 'remember that from this moment, just as you hold my secret, I hold yours.'

He loosens his hold and turns my hands over in his, and sits, stroking a finger gently, so gently, over my palms...

The clock strikes and breaks my thoughts. I find my hands clasped tight together, the joints stiff and painful, and could wish for a gentle caress to sooth the pain away. Looking out through the window I see the driveway shining in the moonlight, waiting, waiting, as I wait for the master of Thornfield Hall to return.

20

DRAWING ROOM

It was late when he returned. He dismounted and without a word flung the reins at John who, shrugging at his master's morose manner, led Mesrour round to the stable yard.

Mr. Rochester stood stock still for a long moment as I watched him closely from my place in the doorway. He was, it seemed to me, shrunken, diminished. Even muffled up against the weather as he was, I could see that he had lost weight. His shoulders sagged as he looked towards the orchard where the brittle outlines of the bent fruit trees were etched starkly against the white sheet of the snow.

He peered forward through the moonlit air, as if he had caught sight of something, someone, moving there among the trees. Did he, too, see a visitant from the past, I wondered. Did he search for her, hurt and happiness twisted together in his mind?

After a time I saw him shake his head and turn slowly round in a full circle, looking first in the direction of the stable yard, then towards the park gate, the laurel walk and the terrace. After that his gaze moved upwards, towards the battlemented roof line, the mullioned windows of the fateful third storey and finally down, until his eyes rested on me at my place by the door.

For a moment it was as if he did not recollect who I was. Then, with a barely audible greeting, he strode towards me muttering some words which I could not make out before, with a suddenly defiant look, he pushed the door wide open with his boot and entered the Hall.

When he eventually summoned me to the Drawing Room and spoke to me, some hours later, he surprised me with the orders he gave. I had imagined that he would want to flee from Thornfield Hall as soon as possible and take refuge in distractions on the Continent.

However, it quickly became clear to me that he had no intention of quitting the Hall, hateful though the place had been to him hitherto.

'Save for a couple of visits to Millcote—' he paused, remembering no doubt those excursions and his wish to lavish a trousseau on his intended bride, 'save for those visits, I never saw her in any other setting than here at Thornfield Hall and its immediate environs.' He stopped speaking abruptly and sought the half-empty brandy decanter which stood on the table beside his chair. He replenished his glass, drank deeply and resumed, speaking in a rapid, repressed undertone. 'She is here in spirit, here, just as surely as *Mrs. Rochester,*' the words hissed between his teeth, 'is here in body.'

I waited. What reply could I make?

'Do you not see her, Mrs. Fairfax?' He suddenly addressed me, his voice so quiet I had difficulty in making out his words. 'Here she is, here, perched on the footstool. She has her pencil in her little hand and her brown head bends over her sketch book.'

He fell silent again but after a pause he looked at me and spoke clearly enough, though his eyes bore a fevered eagerness. 'You see her, don't you, Mrs. Fairfax? Tell me you see her too?'

I shook my head. Such fancies are no solace for the sad at heart. I understand that too well to lie to him.

For a second or two I thought he would rise and strike me for my contradiction, but his hand was raised only to point a denouncing finger at me. '*You* have driven her away!' he exclaimed. 'She was here with me until you sat down. I saw her. I saw her, here, just here.'

He lowered his arm and his great brown hand hovered so gently, so tenderly, a few inches above the side of his chair; it tore my heart to see his fingers caressing the empty air for a brief moment.

Distressed by his distress, and fearing that I should prove to be more harm than help to him by my presence, I was about to make some excuse to enable me to leave the library when he addressed some questions to me about Mrs. Poole and her patient, and I was obliged to supply answers. Even as I spoke, however, his mind wandered. He drank deeply once more and I began to be anxious for him. He has always had a strong head for liquor but fagged, distraught, bereft as he was, I feared that his constitution could not stand such rough treatment.

Eventually he sat so still that I thought he had fallen into a doze. I was about to ease my rheumatic joints out of my chair when he suddenly roused himself, speaking clearly and collectedly.

'Tomorrow morning you are to dismiss Cook, Betsey, Leah and all the outdoor servants,' he stated.

I must have looked as surprised as I felt, because he added, 'Thornfield Hall needs few attendants now. Between them, John and Mary can keep stable and kitchen in order. Mrs. Poole's service is, of course, essential. Tell all the others they shall leave with an extra six months' wages.'

That was a handsome gesture I reckoned, which would go some way to soften the blow of sudden dismissal.

'As to references, you will write them in my name tomorrow morning giving, without exception, unqualified recommendations. Each one of them has served me well.'

I was about to make some comment, suggest that he might reflect awhile before dispensing with his loyal servants so expeditiously, but he waved me aside.

'No demur. It is decided. Leave me now, Mrs. Fairfax. Leave me with my thoughts,' and he strode suddenly across to the window seat, a searching gaze shadowing his face again.

It was not my place to question or disobey. I left the room as quickly and quietly as I might. The new cushion covers, I thought, looked very well in the lamplight. He had never noticed them, of course.

21

SERVANTS' HALL

I was occupied the whole of this morning in penning the letters requested by Mr. Rochester. I did not relish the task and found many pretexts to procrastinate. Once I had begun, I dawdled over details, writing more and more slowly, prolonging the whole business and deferring the time when I would have to speak to all the dismissed servants in turn.

Mrs. Wardle, the cook, has only been with us for four or five years, and so I spoke to her first. I found her on her own, enjoying a quiet cup of tea in the servants' hall in a lull between the finish of luncheon and the start of preparations for the evening meal. She heard me out and replied immediately, saying that she had been considering giving me notice for a month or more, so quiet and dreary a life it was at Thornfield Hall since the master had ridden off on his wild-goose chase. And now that he was back again he did not look as if he would be doing much entertaining, though a butler or cellar-man might be useful to him, she added with a sniff. I ignored her impertinence and let her talk on. She had heard that the cook at Colonel Dent's house was wanting to move south to be near her only son. She would apply there. She believed the Dents kept a comfortable house and did plenty of entertaining. It would suit Mrs. Wardle well. She wound up by saying that she was sure I could have no objection to her leaving the kitchen and pantry and store cupboards as they were. She wanted to start her packing immediately and hoped to leave in the morning. Pocketing her letter and bank notes, she scuttled from the room without a backward glance, eager to be on her way. I doubt she will find the time to bid me a formal farewell before she leaves Thornfield Hall.

Somewhat emboldened by Mrs. Wardle's pragmatic response to the change in her fortunes, I asked John to assemble the gardener, the stable lad and all the other outdoor staff in the servant's hall. I would break the news to them all together.

In the event they too accepted their dismissal calmly, and their remuneration as if it were their due. The general feeling was, I gathered from their few comments, that they would be glad to leave a place where their master no longer took any interest in the estate, and where a mad woman, imprisoned for so long, might, should there be any opportunity, cause injury, distress and danger to anyone in the vicinity.

I noticed Betsey watching as the men left the hall so I called her into my parlour straight away and told her as gently as I could that she was dismissed. She burst out crying almost before the words left my mouth, and with all her sniffling and blubbering I was hard pressed to make out what she said of younger brothers and sisters and a wastrel father and sending money home. I begged her to be composed and dry her tears, and promised that I would do all in my power to see her settled into some good position as soon as might be. I thought it would cheer her to hear what I had written about her and, although she was still gulping and sniffing when I started to read out her letter of recommendation, she soon began to listen attentively, and the colour rose in her cheeks and a smile returned to her lips when she heard the favourable terms in which her character was presented. Her smile grew broader when I named the sum of money she was promised in lieu of notice. In minutes she was quite restored to her usual good-humoured self, rattling on about how she would now be able to fulfil her ambition to become a lady's maid. Ever since Miss Mary Ingram had shown her some favour last spring, requesting that Betsey alone should be entrusted with the ironing of her dresses, she had dreamt of elevating herself from her position as housemaid. Now it seemed the opportunity had arisen. Would I write a letter to Ingram Park, she begged, inquiring as to whether a position should be available for her there? She hoped, she confided in me as she was about to leave the room, that Giles, the Ingram's under-footman might still be in the family's employ. Warning her not to place her hopes too firmly on Ingram Park or its footman, I said I would make the necessary enquiries and in the meantime she should prepare to visit her family for a few days. She left my parlour with quite a spring in her step.

All day I had been delaying an interview with Leah. She came here as a timid girl of some twelve years old, just a short while after I was widowed and became Thornfield Hall's housekeeper. I remember her then as a slight, pale little thing who took to her work dutifully and who blossomed when I praised her. I have grown fond of her over the years and I know that, her family living at some distance, Thornfield has become home to her. How would she take my news?

Like Betsey she wept at first, and like all the servants she soon began to think of her future. She told me that she did not want to move far away from Thornfield but hoped that Millcote would provide an opportunity for her. Perhaps the Rochester Arms required a chambermaid. She would try there first. I wondered if her plans, like Betsey's, were motivated by interests of the heart as much as by convenience or necessity.

So my unpleasant duty was executed with less trouble than I anticipated. And while Mrs. Wardle, Betsey and Leah are all busy packing up their belongings, their lives turned upside down and their minds on what the future may hold, I sit comfortably at my parlour fireside, thinking over the events of the past months and years. Visitants drive up to Thornfield's great doorway, alight and glide into its chambers and along its passageways; the oaken panels absorb their voices, questioning, recounting, responding, and release them back to me like measured breathing; laughter and cries seep into the softness of cushions and curtains; the very wainscots and shutters hold its history.

I believe I shall sleep.

22

PARLOUR

I am shocked at what I have written, finding it hard to believe that I even know such words, and I scrunch the paper up in my hand, concealing its offensiveness.

I lift my pen and try again, suppressing emotion, focussing attention on essentials.

> *My Dear Cousin Sarah,*
>
> *You will be surprised, no doubt, to hear from me after all these years and I trust that you will not be affronted that I write to you now after so long a silence. I would not trouble you with communication except that there is no one else in the world to whom I can turn.*

Will that do? Will she think I use her, care not for her? Remembering her of old, I know she can be quick to take exception, has been known to harden her heart against me. As children our connection was tenuous, the blood tie alone holding us loosely together in place of a bond of true friendship. And I remember that I neglected her sadly once Rowland strode into my life, abandoning girlish entertainments when he beckoned.

I should start my letter again but I lack the energy. And I care little whether she is irked or no. Either she will take me in or she will not. It matters not to me. I must live somewhere, I suppose, but I cannot picture where it will be or how I will fare.

Some time has passed. I stare at the paper, see that there are scratches close ribbed across the leather edge of my writing slope. I must have scraped my pen there, time and again. I do not remember doing that.

It is quite spoilt.

The tears are standing in my eyes. My beautiful writing desk is damaged and that grieves me. The scratched leather is like torn skin and I run my finger over it, as if to seal up a wound.

Once more I dip my pen in ink and resume my writing.

> *My position as housekeeper at Thornfield Hall is terminated after more than eleven years' devoted service, and I find myself, at approaching fifty years of age, homeless and alone.*

There is nothing to be gained by subtlety. I have stated the fact baldly. I continue without pausing.

> *You may assure yourself that no untoward behaviour of mine has caused this sudden and unexpected reversal of my fortunes. I can only assume that my master's wits are tainted, for he has cast off all his servants except for the groom and his wife, deluding himself, I'll be bound, that they can render all service that he will require in the future. Mr. Rochester's morose nature and independent habits have hardened into downright eccentricity in recent weeks and – I tremble to pen the words – his drinking has increased to a level I consider dangerous to himself and to those about him.*
>
> *Consequently, my dear Cousin, I write to throw*

myself on your mercy and trust that your charitable, benevolent sensitivities will persuade you to come to my aid. As my only surviving relative, I beg (see how I am reduced from independent status to importunity) to be allowed to make my home with you and your kind husband. I ask only for shelter and companionship for a few weeks or months until I can make other, more permanent, arrangements if you feel unable to open your door as a permanent asylum to me.

It only remains for me to mention that my former employer has left me very well provided for and that I am therefore in a position to fund my own needs without bringing any financial burden to you, your husband or your home.

Believe me, my dear Sarah, your troubled, unhappy and homeless cousin,

Alice Elizabeth Fairfax.

23

HAY LANE

My letter is posted. Nothing now to do but wait. Wait for a reply. Whatever it will be.

I rub my hands together to try and keep them warm. I am surprised to find that I have come out without my gloves. It is very cold. My footsteps make a strange, eerie squeaking as I negotiate the deep-packed snow on Hay Lane. At my every step words throb in my head – 'I must go elsewhere, elsewhere, somewhere, wherever.' I try to beat their sense into my brain. But their meaning slips away even as I pace.

I am weary. Very soon now it will be my fiftieth birthday. And for all but six months of my life I have always been within sight of Hay Lane and Thornfield Hall.

And now I must go elsewhere, elsewhere, somewhere, wherever.

I stifle my grief by stoking up my anger. I am cast out, discarded, thrown away like a dirty duster; an unwanted, broken chattel. My loyalty and my devotion count for nothing. I am disregarded.

The black bars of the bare tree trunks stretch beside me along the avenue.

I am a little breathless and I halt, look upwards. Above me, fingertips of twigs bend towards each other, touch, so gently in the slightest breath of a breeze. No other movement. Silence. Emptiness.

I resume my walk. Now, at the fringed edge of earshot there is a voice pleading

> …'Wait for me. Wait for me…'
> And I answer, 'Take my hand.'

I have said the words aloud to no one. I look about me. There is no one to speak; no one to hear. Silence. Emptiness.

What was it Sarah and I used to chant, in childhood?

> … *'Talk to yourself and all will see, You're turning mad as mad can be!'*

Mentally I reprimand myself. Keep control; guard your composure. You know that you can do so. You wrote a clear letter to Cousin Sarah. You used none of the dreadful words that you scrawled on first sheet of paper when you were so broken, so angry, wounded as surely as if a knife had sliced your skin. Walk steadily back. Resume your position (while you have it) as housekeeper of Thornfield Hall. Walk briskly home now, before it gets dark.

Home.

I no longer have a claim to the place I have called my home.

And suddenly I need to be back there in my parlour, by my fireside, savouring its comfort and tranquillity while it is still mine. Not wasting elsewhere any moment which can be spent there. While it is still mine.

I take my own advice and my heart lifts a little as I near the Hall.

But at the edge of the laurel walk a lurch of panic hits me from nowhere and I have to lean on the stone gate post to save myself from falling. My letter to Cousin Sarah! It is posted now, starting its journey to Kidderminster. Gone from my hand, out of my reach and control.

And on which sheet of paper is it written?

Despite logicality and sense, I see myself folding up the first, scrawled, blasphemous words which dripped unbidden from my pen, like pus from an infected wound, addressing it, carrying it, handing it over at Millcote post office. And I also see the plain, respectable request for asylum lying forgotten on my writing slope.

Pushing my aching bones into action I break into a run and, careless of ice or snow or uneven pathway, I chase across the terrace, stumble to the entrance, fling open the front door and hurry to the sanctuary of my parlour—

—where I find the blotted, angry outpourings lying crumpled, harmless where I left them.

The laughter of relief bubbles into my throat, upwards into my mouth, and floats round the room like soap suds frothed by a whirling hand on washing day. I bite my fist to squash mirth down, and then I scratch out, obliterate, the worst words, time and again, until the paper shreds and tatters and, still laughing oh so quietly to myself, I drop the fragments into the hearth.

24

STILL ROOM

It is but two days since, her arrangements having been finalised satisfactorily, little Leah and I said our farewell, and in those forty-eight hours what a bustle I have been in. No sooner had the aspiring chamber maid left than a letter from my cousin Sarah was delivered to me. She wrote less kindly than I might have hoped and more speedily than I could have wished (for I would stay here longer were I free to do so) but she and her husband have offered a place in their home to me 'for as long a period of time as may be expedient and desirable to the three of us.' Heaven knows, I am not in any position to reject her offer.

Once again my life is prescribed for me by events outside my control. Once again, necessity forces me to accept upheaval and removal as benevolence.

Sarah's letter contains numerous reiterated remarks concerning the costs of running a large house. From these I infer that, her husband having this year been unable to visit his chambers in consequence of ill health, the couple appear to be suffering pecuniary difficulties. Perhaps my financial independence and my many years' experience as housekeeper of a large establishment may prove helpful to her in her terraced town house. I trust she will be grateful for any advice I can offer.

As to Leah, the dear girl looked sorry to leave me and pressed a little paper-wrapped gift into my hand which, in my busyness, I have not yet had the opportunity to open. For all her tears I could see that she was thrilled at the prospect of taking up her position at the Rochester Arms. As she set off, her scant belongings piled up on the cart beside her, I felt a cold pang of loneliness. While I remained at Thornfield Hall I knew I could expect no friendliness from taciturn Mrs. Poole, little company from John and Mary whose duties are much more onerous now than when a number of servants were employed here, and no notice at all from Mr. Rochester himself. Since his return he has barely moved from his private quarters.

I set to, therefore, to pack up my belongings after, with a certain perverse pride, I had ensured that everything was in order as to the furnishings of the house and in the contents of its store cupboards, still rooms, cellars and pantries. I would have asked the master for permission to take some bottles of blackcurrant cordial and sloe gin from the still room as gifts for my cousin and her husband, but he would not answer his door when I knocked and called out for permission to enter. Since he uttered the terms of my dismissal we have not exchanged a word.

In the hall way my trunks stand packed and corded and all my boxes, save a final one, are secured, each with its card of address nailed on. It only remains for me to help myself to such comestibles as may be acceptable to my new host and hostess.

But are they to be host and hostess and am I to be their guest? Or are they to be my landlords and I their lodger? Is it possible or likely that I should call them friends? As ever I find myself in an indeterminate position and in a situation very different from one which I might have hoped for. When the order came to give notice to the servants here I imagined, if I had any conscious thoughts at all, that I would remain at Thornfield Hall until the end of my days; a trusted confidante, a valued mistress of the house, respectable, reliable, needed.

The pain of disappointment and rejection does not fade. It smoulders still.

I struggle a little with the bottles, taking three at a time, and return to the still room for some preserves and pickles that Sarah may well enjoy. I am about my business when I see the heavy form of Grace Poole in the doorway. We exchange a few words. She knows I am to leave but does not enquire about my new position. Nor does she wish me well for my future or for the start of my journey tomorrow. The best she can do is to say that she believes the snow will return and that I would do well to be off betimes.

So contrary she seems, standing there as solid as a sideboard, her plain face set like a figure in a nursery rhyme or children's fable, that her grudging concern for my welfare amuses me and I laugh out loud. No doubt she thinks I am happy to be leaving Thornfield Hall and her knowing look and her misconception strike me as ludicrous. To stop myself bellowing with laughter in her face, I turn to the stone shelving and lift down a heavy pitcher of my best sloe gin. I hand it to her, telling her it is a farewell present. I hope she will enjoy it, she and her charge, too.

Maybe, I think, it will warm their loneliness in their realm at the top of this great gloomy old house.

She gives me a nod and takes the pitcher from me with a half smile and makes her way aloft.

I close and lock the still-room door. There. All is done. I am finished. I have said farewell to Mary and early tomorrow morning John will drive me to Millcote where I will await the stagecoach. Mr. Rochester has instructed John to use the carriage rather than the cart for my last journey. That is the extent of his farewell to me. Just that much consideration is accorded me, I, who long ago believed I was loved by one master of Thornfield Hall, and thought, years later, that I was valued above the commonplace by another.

25

THE LEADS

It is not so much dawn as a slackening of night. Something has awoken me.

Perhaps it was the front door opening or closing. Was it? Has my master, sleepless, restless as he always is, gone out into the stillness, searching in the thin mist for the slight figure of the governess? Has he caught a glimpse of something moving among the shadows cast by the full moon? Does he imagine she has returned?

I lie awake listening. But no, I can hear nothing now.

Nor can I sleep again. I am wide awake. It is as if I am to savour every second of my last few hours here, no moment to be dribbled away in dozing. I light my lamp, pour water from ewer into bowl, wash and dress myself. I fold my night clothes and place them with my slippers in the carpet bag at the foot of my bed.

There is nothing else for me to do. It has struck five and John will be ready for me before six. I am about to quit my chamber and go down to the kitchen to drink and eat a little before my journey, when once again I am alerted by some sound.

It is somewhere above me. A door opening and closing with

a creak of hinges. God forbid that it should be the poor maniac up to some mischief, as has occurred before. I stand stock still, unblinking, hardly breathing and can hear – nothing!

Gradually my pattering heartbeat slackens and rationality returns. Mrs. Rochester's previous nightly excursions have habitually been accompanied by manic laughter, by shrieks and screams and howls, I recall. Now, however, in this fragile dawn, all is quiet. Most likely I hear Mrs. Poole about her business, securing a door here, tending to her patient there. Or can it be that the master himself has ventured aloft to see how she fares? He has, in his rough manner, sometimes shown concern for the woman he married, never raising a hand to her, for all her wildness. And in the past he made careful provision for her well-being; that I can vouch for.

But now? Since he fell under the governess's enchantment, and since her disappearance, how can his actions be accounted for or accredited? Is it possible that by cutting himself off as he has done from all normal human intercourse, and by drinking by the hour in solitary misery, his wits may have become as deranged as those of his spouse? Does he now roam the hall at night time, intent on harm to her or others?

No. I cannot think it of him. More likely he is a danger to himself, poor man. He may well have ignored me, disregarded me, forgotten my very existence during these last days, but I could wish to do him one last service before we are irrevocably parted. If he has need of any support or succour, I will find him out and offer it now.

Taking my lamp I climb the stairs and, as I make my way along the narrow third floor corridor, I feel a sudden cold draught ruffling my hair. I look up and am surprised to see the hatch-way to the roof aslant, partly open, a grey wedge of sky dimly visible. Someone is up there on the leads, or has been there very recently.

Trembling, but unable to turn back, I place the lamp beside the wooden framework of the aperture and haul myself up. Suppressing the surge of memories of my other excursions here, I tentatively step out, peering about me in the gloaming, hoping or dreading, I am uncertain which, to find who is waiting up here.

I stand, the silence almost palpable, stretching towards me. I feel as if I am being watched, but I force myself to turn right around, scanning northwards, east, south and west. I can see no one.

Straining my ears, it seems for a second as though a voice far, far away, is calling to me, pleading, 'Come to me! Hold me! Help me!' It may be begging but it slides away even as I catch its breathy whispering and I fear that it speaks only in my head.

Either my eyes are becoming accustomed to the flickering moonlight, or the darkness is thinning. I make out notches of crenellations, black against the slab of sky. A chimney stack to my left casts blocks of shadow at my feet and there, there, beside the brickwork, what is it? who is it? lying there half hidden in a smothering cloak or shroud-like blanket.

I take two steps forward, peering to see more clearly, and the shape slides away and forms itself into dusky shadows.

Now I am suddenly, horribly, frightened, as much by what is not up here on the leads as by what I had thought might be. In the last few weeks I have so frequently heard voices speaking to me, and have often times seen figures fade into nothingness as I approached them, vanishing into the woodland, beside the door way, along the lane. They trouble me and sadden me, these slippery visitations. I want no more of them. I turn and run to the hatchway, not stooping for my lamp, caring for nothing but to get away, get away, from the wraiths which will come to me and trick me, will conceal themselves from me and laugh at me as they play their tormenting games of hide and seek.

Back in the safety of my bed chamber I fling the door shut and lean against it, struggling to get my breath. My heart is racing again and my head spins. The embers of the fire glow like a half-closed eye and I stumble over the carpet to scatter sticks and armfuls of kindling into the grate until the flames jump up and a comforting light dances across the room.

Dizzy and faint, I sink to my knees on the hearth rug, feeling in my pocket for my salts bottle and find my fingers clutching instead a soft, tissue-paper wrapped parcel. It has been there, forgotten, since Leah's departure, more than two full days ago.

The dear girl! I stroke the white paper. It rustles under my fingers. A little gift from the housemaid. And I had forgotten all about it. I am glad she does not know of my forgetfulness; it would have seemed like an unkindness to her.

Carefully, almost with reverence, I undo the ribbon with which the parcel is tied, unfold the paper and find within, two small squares of white lawn. Pocket handkerchiefs! Each is neatly hemmed in Leah's fine stitching. She has taken trouble with them, made them for me herself. A thoughtful gift.

I am about to re-wrap them and place them in my carpet bag when something catches my eye and I lean forward, close to the crackling fire to see more clearly. There is appliqué work in a corner of each handkerchief. A flower has been meticulously cut from some piece of linen and daintily stitched there.

A daisy.

A daisy! It dances before my eyes as if it grew in a field and blew in the wind. I know every stitch of its pattern, every stitch which my own fingers traced during that sad, empty winter while I watched and waited at Ferndean Manor.

I struggle to frame the thought coherently, though its truth has stabbed my brain as sure and swift and dangerous as a lightning bolt. Leah is my child. My Dorothea. My gift – returned and lost to me in the same instant.

The tears flood my eyes and I cry, there on the hearth rug, cry for lost motherhood and for a cheating fate and for long years of emptiness. I cry for my rectitude and my respectability which I wore like a snail carrying its shell, setting a barrier between the world around me and the softness of my heart. I cry for the opportunities and possibilities which have eluded me.

I weep for the imagined sweetness of a daughter's smile. My winsome daughter with her warm brown eyes, slender as a flower in her sweet mauve dress …

And beneath me, within me, around me, overwhelming the bitterness of my self-pity, out of that picture in my mind's eye another truth jumps at me like a wild creature, jolts me with a physical force which takes the breath from my body.

I hear Joan Mudge humming to herself in the stable doorway. I see Leah-Dorothea raising her arms to shake a white tablecloth. I see the hot breath rising from Jem's lips...

There are no words I can frame. Groaning, I rock myself back and forth, back and forth, clamping my lips together, clutching my arms tight around my body to keep the dreadful thought from escaping. I want to beat out the past and the future with my fists, here, here on the very hearth rug, obliterate the empty worthlessness which has been my life.

Suddenly it is all more than I can bear. My thoughts are in turmoil but one thing I know: I must get away, get away from Thornfield Hall and its master and its secrets, its poisoned memories and its mockery of motherhood.

I cannot bear the white softness of the handkerchiefs in my hand and, as if they are live things which could harm me, I throw the little lawn squares into the fire. I toss ribbon and wrappings after them, upturn the wood basket, scatter logs, kindling and sticks to hide them, cover them, to bury them under the flames.

26

THE DRIVE

The trunks are stowed and the manservant places the last of the boxes inside the carriage at the lady's feet. She holds her carpet bag tightly in her gloved hand. She looks her age, the man thinks, as he closes the door and climbs up to his seat. She's neat enough as always, her merino-trimmed wrapper cinched at her chin. Her bonnet is edged in merino too and her kid gloves are buttoned with mother-of-pearl. Her skirt is fine wool and her boots look new. She's not had to stint herself, that's for sure. No doubt she has put away a tidy little sum over the years. And she's been here longer than the rest of us. But she aged this autumn. Perhaps a change of scene will do her good.

He gathers reins and whip and clicks his teeth. 'Trot on, Topper,' he calls and the dun gelding makes off down the familiar driveway.

The lady is dry eyed but her composure is brittle as glass. She fixes her eyes on the house, turning her head to keep the mansion in sight for the length of the drive. Near the gateway she raps on the roof, calling out, 'Stop a minute, if you please, John.'

The driver does as he is bidden and waits, the horse's breath rising in the chilly dawn light.

The lady lets down the window and cranes her neck forward for one last look at Thornfield Hall.

A long moment passes before she instructs the driver to continue on their way. As the horse picks up speed and the mansion fades into the distance, it seems to her that the first rosy light of sunrise is fingering its way across the window of the room that had been her bedchamber, flickering and glowing there as the carriage bears her away.

***

About the Author

The daughter of a West Riding woollen manufacturer and the silent movie child star, Twinkles Hunter who played the young Cathy in the 1920 film of 'Wuthering Heights', Anna Bransgrove has lived in Yorkshire for most of her life.

While working in secondary schools as an English and Drama teacher she directed numerous musicals and straight plays, many of them presented at the Stephen Joseph Theatre in the Round, Scarborough. Shortlisted in 2011 in the first short story competition of the National Association of Writers' Groups, she was commended by Dame Margaret Drabble in the Brontë Society's creative writing competition in 2014.

Anna and her husband, Michael, have two sons, five grandchildren, run an antiques business, and live in Hull and Correze.

Lightning Source UK Ltd.
Milton Keynes UK
UKOW05f1018111016

284986UK00015B/247/P